Aug 2021

MATT FITZPATRICK
**MATRIARCH
GAME**

Corey,

Enjoy

Mutt

ALSO BY MATT FITZPATRICK

Crosshairs: *A Justin McGee Novel*

A JUSTIN MCGEE NOVEL

MATT FITZPATRICK

MATRIARCH GAME

GREEN PLACE BOOKS | *Brattleboro, Vermont*

Printed in the United States

10 9 8 7 6 5 4 3 2 1

GREEN WRITERS PRESS is a Vermont-based publisher whose mission is to spread a
message of hope and renewal through the words and images we publish. Throughout
we will adhere to our commitment to preserving and protecting the natural resources of
the earth. To that end, a percentage of our proceeds will be donated to environmental
activist groups and the author's focus on preserving the Cape Cod seashore. Green
Writers Press gratefully acknowledges support from individual donors, friends, and
readers to help support the environment and our publishing initiative.
GREEN PLACE BOOKS curates books that tell literary and compelling stories
with a focus on writing about place.

GREEN
PLACE
BOOKS

Giving Voice to Writers & Artists Who Will Make the World a Better Place

Green Writers Press | Brattleboro, Vermont
www.greenwriterspress.com

ISBN: 978-1-950584-50-5

COVER DESIGN: Asha Hossain Design LLC

For information, please contact the author at mfitz71@comcast.net

The paper used in this publication is produced by mills committed
to responsible and sustainable forestry practices.

I want to kindly send a cordial invitation for you to return to the tumultuous world of attorney and assassin, Justin McGee.

As you will see, much has and will change with the exception of the unpredictable and unorthodox events that invade his hurricane life.

Some of the characters in the following pages you will recognize from the world of Crosshairs, but I did offer an introduction to a new group of flawed personas.

Shake well, and enjoy with a twist.

—Bassing Harbor, Cape Cod, Late Fall 2019

"Image is an eyeless game."

— Neil Peart

"And a child shall lead them…"

— Isaiah 11:6

In memory of William S. Rizos, my best friend and brother.

Not a day goes by when I don't hear your infectious laughter...

MATT FITZPATRICK
MATRIARCH GAME

The vessel Free Lance
(almost one year ago)

The austere judge loudly cleared her throat as a signal for all present in the Barnstable County, Cape Cod courtroom to now be silent.

"The People versus Justin S. McGee will now commence."

Justin, accompanied by his attorney and former law firm partner, staggered as he approached the front of the court.

Her Honor continued.

"Mr. McGee, the alleged charges are of the highest level of severity. Murder-one in broad daylight, in the presence of children, is tantamount to being accused of conspiring with Satan himself."

Slowly, blood began to seep out of the judge's eyes and started to drip, only to disappear in the endless black of her robe.

"Dead, dead, dead! Mr. McGee, do you understand the finality of that word? I fear you do not."

Justin hiccuped as his counsel tried to politely interrupt the judge.

"Your honor, may we please continue with the arraignment. Mr. McGee is innocent until proven guilty, and honestly your sanguinary eyes are most unnerving to the jurors."

The judge's eyes were now a crimson sieve.

"Fuck you counselor, and those zombies in the jury box! I make the rules here. I, and only I, will decide the fate of Mr. McGee. To hell with the jury and their pathetic existences. Who has such idle time that they can cough up six months to serve on a murder gig. I own Justin McGee. McGee, do you hear me? If you actually had a soul, I would swallow it and spit it out as black embers."

The court presider hissed, "However, perhaps we do have a jury who is willing and able to efficiently convict this thief of innocent lives.

"In addition McGee, you execute your victims in a most cowardly fashion. No, you do not look them in the eye. No, you do not stand face to face in a caged octagon.

"Instead, you shoot them in cold blood from hundreds of yards away, often taking them out in front of loved ones and innocent bystanders. Are you proud of yourself McGee?! Are you?! Fucking snake. Coward. Liar. COWARD!"

Justin gazed over to his right side toward the jury box that was barely noticeable seconds ago, only to now find that the box was chock full of disturbing remnants of people with wounds and blood covering their ghostly gray-skinned faces.

Jus immediately recognized them as past assignments. He then stepped forward, only to stumble and be helped back up by his lawyer.

The judge screamed, "The nerve of you Mr. McGee. To murder! To strike down in cold blood the woman you supposedly loved! To show no remorse, and moreover to stand before our forum drunk as a sailor on a Singapore shore leave. Officers, I've had enough of the sight of this sinner before me. Take him away and let him rot while he awaits the worms!"

The judge slammed down her gavel, only it wasn't a wooden implement, but rather her right hand shaped into a metal pirate's hook that smashed the top of the large wooden desk.

Justin, in his state of alcohol-induced impairment merely stood and swayed. He did not speak, but rather just watched the unsightly jury box horror.

The court officers grabbed him in order to shackle his hands and feet. He thrust his arms out awaiting the cuffs, but the burlier of the *two officers grabbed Justin's hands and placed them by his side as he was shackled to his waist.*

The judge continued, "Enjoy your time in prison. We'll try your case in a so-called court of law someday. In the interim, enjoy 20 1/2 out of every 24 hours locked in your cell. But fear not of possible solitary confinement. I would not want you to be alone. Would Marlene Dunn wish you to be alone? No, you will be bunkmates with the one they call 'Tripod', and that's not due to his proficiency in photography. Enjoy your stay. I shall perhaps call your trial in a few months when I stop this damned bleeding."

The blood stopped seeping from the Judge's eyes, only to find a more convenient escape route via her mouth. Justin, in some twisted way felt a humorous moment and almost chuckled, as he watched the judge sport her best Gene Simmons pose.

Justin once again looked to his right at the chaotic jury box now teeming full of the most grotesque creatures that he had ever seen. Oozing wounds, dried dirt and bloodstains covered their ghastly gray body shapes. Despite their horrific appearance, Justin easily recognized his former marks. They certainly recognized him, as they kept chanting in a haunting tone, "Justin. Coward. Justin. Liar!"

Justin couldn't stop looking as he noticed them one by one. The first was Irish wanna-be gangster, Crasha Maloney, whose siren-like dimples were now weighted down by clots of blood. Crasha held the hubris that because of her distant relation to an underworld boss, it gave her license to murder in Boston with impunity.

Hunched over next to Crasha was the Jamaican gold purveyor from that desolate pop-up town on the dark road to Negril. The incessant blanket of ganja fog prevented him from understanding that to threaten the life of Justin McGee was a crime that one only had a single chance to commit. He ended up alone and disemboweled in the island brush.

Even the Orthodox Jew who was simply dubbed "Target" sat in the jury box with his head streaming blood with a hand dug into his maroon matted hair. Before Jus ended his victim's career, Target forsook the wise teachings and business practices of his father, and blazed a different career path that was paved with deceit and violence. Justin's assignment called for Target to be taken out in front of his family who were poolside on a particularly pleasant South Florida afternoon.

And finally there was Matilda Chong, whose head rested on the jury box rail, while her long, raven hair hung toward the floor as if from a hangman's noose. She slowly looked up and sported half a row of smiling teeth, for the other half of her head was missing. Matilda was a jilted lover who had the audacity to manipulate the market value of her lesbian partner's family business empire. Such a violation was clearly noticed and would not be committed without commensurate punishment via Justin's rifle scope.

He saw them all, and each one yearned to take a gnashing bite out of his Hell-awaiting soul.

Jus didn't know if it was the horror of the scene or pure alcohol withdrawal symptoms, but he suddenly felt saliva pooling in his mouth. He vomited violently on the courtroom floor a retched sight of bile and undeterminable stomach contents. He felt dizzy and weak, and could only hear the taunts and jeers from the Hell-spawned jury box. With a quick flash, Jus fell into a full-blown, thrashing withdrawal seizure on the courtroom floor and blacked out. The last thing he remembered was the sight of the courtroom ceiling, and the numbness of his self-mutilated tongue which tasted of old copper.

When he came to a few minutes later, his clothes and hair were sopping with his own vomit. Blood from his tongue wounds oozed from his mouth as a reminder of the violent spasm. All around him was noise, screaming and even saw-blade laughter.

While dazed and having only faint feeling in his body, he did sense a slight tug on his left foot. He ignored it at first, but then looked down only to notice the silky, almond-colored half-face of Matilda Chong. During his seizure, she had managed to fall out of jury box and thumped onto the filthy courtroom floor. She then crawled over to Justin's limp body, and proceeded to calmly gnaw on his big toe.

Finally, he saw Boston Assistant District Attorney, Marlene Dunn, but she was not in the jury box. Instead, her ghostly white apparition approached the bench and stood next to a now completely blood-soaked judge. Marl patted her honor on the shoulder, dabbed her blood-spewing mouth with her middle finger, and proceeded to take a lick while uncontrollably starting to chuckle. A most riotous, hearty laugh that revealed deep, scarlet-colored teeth and eyes that slowly dripped pyin.

"Huh - what!!"

"What happened?" Justin repeatedly whispered in machine gun tones to the empty master stateroom on his live-aboard boat. But he already knew the answer to his own question, for the nightmare often visited, and it's frequent appearances never lost their acute level of disturbance.

Justin shot open his eyes, sat up in his bed and slowly extricated himself from the brutal memories of the frequent dream. In the nightmare, his soul was damned, which perhaps was the case in the real world as well.

Jus had never been prone to nightmares, for he didn't need to be. The mental knife wounds created by the memories of the assassination of the woman he loved wreaked so much havoc in his mind, that the recurring dreams were merely shoulder taps.

"She's dead," he muttered to himself. While he had pulled the trigger, and witnessed the shattering explosion of Marlene Dunn on the steps of Boston's Moakley Courthouse, she still lived in the dungeons of his guilty mind. The memories feasted and sated on the endless buffet served by the assassin's remorse.

He walked into the vessel's master head and stared at himself in the mirror, thinking how amazing it was that despite making national headlines, with a little hair grown out and immediately dyed blonde, that nobody had ever recognized him. The newly grown goatee also contributed to his efforts at anonymity.

He knew that he should feel fortunate, but what nobody would ever understand was the personal Hell in which he lived every day. Despite having donned the Grim Reaper's robe and sickle many times, he had never learned to live with the after effects of what he had done to Marlene. He had shared her laughter and tasted her breath.

As a result of his ultimate betrayal, he now constantly heard voices, sirens, and the tolling of low-toned bells. He resided inside a sardonic mental pinball machine that was slowly forcing him into a Poe-like state of madness.

Chapter 1

Jekyll Island, GA (six months later)

Justin stared at what had to be a ghost, but the rational part of his brain knew that this was no apparition.

Marlene looked at him with a wry smile, and then remarked, "Hey Jus, you seem to have spilled something on your shirt."

Jus looked down expecting a ketchup stain on his $300 linen button-down, and subsequently he found it.

Only it was bright red and perfectly annular. It was a pronounced scarlet dot that slightly jiggled from side to side when he moved.

And at the moment, the stain was trained precisely on his sternum.

Marlene sported the wide smile of the Cheshire Cat.

Justin McGee could not help but still stare at Marlene Dunn with disbelief and a just seen a ghost set of eyes, yet his fixation did not detract from the attention he was dedicating to the dot resting comfortably on his chest.

"Justin, or is it Tom Baxter these days? You were my lover, my future, and eventually my would-be-killer. Of course, you do realize what that stain on your shirt really is?"

Justin's blank gaze mirrored his inability to respond.

"Speaking of which, you look quite comfortable in your new selection of attire, Mr. Baxter. Brooks Brothers must be boarding up the windows and handing out pink slips?"

Jus tried to remain calm and not show panic, "Marl, my goal is that the next suit and tie I wear will find me horizontal and glimmering in a mahogany shine."

Marl smirked and replied, "Fitting. That day might come sooner than expected."

One should know to tread lightly when a strong woman is running on adrenaline-filled emotion.

Jus quietly accepted the bitter irony of this situation due to his prior occupation. He certainly never envisioned being on this end of that sinister red light, which at first Justin naively believed to be a simple ketchup stain.

Marlene Dunn continued, "Does it suck to be on the bitch end of that glow? And you certainly know from how far that ketchup stain can come from. One hundred yards? Two hundred? You would have more experience with such a calculation. How does it feel?"

Jus rubbed the stubble on his now sweating face.

"Do you feel vulnerable? God forbid that you would ever feel human. Trust when I say that your shirt stain was born roughly 150 yards away. Are you impressed? Would that be up to your professional standards?

"However, at this moment you are indeed human. You're most likely feeling fear for the first time."

Marl relentlessly continued, "Think of it. At any minute, if I so choose, you would bleed like a human. Would feel pain like a human. Would slowly die like a human. All of the above would be the most human-like emotions you've ever felt. Kind of exciting, would you agree?"

Jus stared at the red skittle sniffing around his chest, for it was like a hungry alley rat patiently awaiting a needle-stuck soul to select which end of a dumpster to serve as his final resting place.

Marl continued, "Fine Zegna shirt, Justin. Actually, that fabric is quite efficient for absorbing liquids. Not sure if any of these waitresses or bar staff would even realize that you got run over by a bus full of Instant Karma.

"Actually, in this candlelight on such a beautiful, warm summer evening, I should think that they would figure you might have spilled Malbec on your shirt. I like how it teases a look at your taut chest, which hosts more lies than there are bees in a hive."

Marl continued, "However, I think that the color accessory goes well with your outfit. Maybe we should get you a matching handkerchief? You can wear it while we order an appetizer?"

Jus was now losing his patience, "Enough talk. You didn't come all the way here to bicker like the Golden Girls."

Marlene paused and picked up a cocktail menu, "I've heard that the mojitos are pleasant here. The most authentic north of Miami."

Justin was stunned. He was certainly not used to playing on the defensive side of the ball. He was completely confused at taking the stage in the role of quarry.

"Marl... I don't know what to say. I, I..."

To which Marl responded, "I understand, Jus. Tough to have dinner with a ghost. Not to mention that my name is not Mrs. Muir who you might find staring into a fucking wishing well, and not to mention all the while a certain friend of mine is trained on your chest and is eager to crack it open like a king crab leg, or perhaps we should simply blow out your trachea if I so choose at this moment?

"That particular stain on your shirt shall remain fixed for every second while we are having our discussion. Maybe even longer?

"Justin. You do realize that it is only I, who will decide what to do with your slowly graying-haired skull. Do you fully grasp the fact that one year ago in Boston you attempted, and fortunately failed, to end my life?"

To which Jus replied, "Marl, I did not wish you dead. I was absolutely caught between Scylla and Charybdis. I have no excuse for what I did, but I needed to save Meyer. They were going to kill him, then eventually you and I, if I did not handle this piece of work for very powerful people. Apparently, known to you or not, your snooping around some tech stock scam last year exposed you to some extremely dangerous characters, one in particular named Darby McBride. May I never have the pleasure of his company ever again."

"Well, whatever Jus. I'm glad that you saved Meyer. How is he these days?"

Jus sensed the tension at the table ebbing a bit, "I'm not sure Marl. We agreeably lost touch after that day at the Moakley Courthouse. We thought it best that we part ways and minimize correspondence to protect him from accusations of complicity. I'm sure he's fine. Shit, the guy is the consummate survivor. I haven't heard from him, but I'll reach out soon."

Marl said, "Well, Mr. Baxter, I can save you some valuable time," which immediately confused and alarmed Jus.

"You see, with my injury, the D.A. forced me out of the office on paid leave due to the stress and medical situation, but she secured me a job as the interim Executive Director at the New England Aquarium.

"The deal was that I could still collect full pay and benefits courtesy of the Commonwealth of Massachusetts, which of course the sucker tax-payers continue to front. The chumps will never learn.

"Meyer was found and picked up a few months ago as I was recuperating. He was actually instrumental in helping me track you down. Not that he ratted you out, but we used basic context clues provided by answers to certain questions that were posed to him."

Justin gulped deeply and continued to stare more warily as Marlene continued.

"He was quick to share the fact that you always held an affinity for this snake hole swamp. He also may have been coaxed by the fire brand that we plunged into his left shoulder."

Justin's eyes blew a wide look of shock.

"Oh yeah, and also the one that sizzled on his forehead. That one proved to be most odiferous.

"However, we were grateful to Meyer and got him a job at the Aquarium as a sign of our appreciation. It doesn't pay much, but he seems to be enjoying it. He was always such a damned handsome and intelligent guy. After he inadvertently assisted us in finding you, we felt compelled to give him some steady work at the facility."

Jus responded, "Marl, he is an Olympic-worthy athlete who has dominated the wheelchair division of the Boston Marathon for a number of years. You have him cleaning penguin shit?"

Marl responded, "Jus, may I remind you, my lover and savior, and also wanna-be assassin, that I have way too much admiration for him to ever do that. That would be disrespectful.

"No, Meyer deserved better and we provided him with a proper salary with commensurate benefits, as we genuinely felt obligated.

"We would never ask a disabled veteran, so smart and strong, to feed the dolphins or the seals, for the sheer monotony would prove maddening. We wanted to be fair for his helping lead us to you."

"Shit." Jus thought aloud. "Did Meyer really know where I went on the lam?"

Marl continued, "Not exactly, Jus. And he was forever loyal to you. Such a great guy."

Marl flipped her hair, "Anyway, the Aquarium acquired a sizable grant from some Metro-West twit Save the Whales type, who finally realized that the whales are pretty much fucked due to all of the political red tape and public apathy, and that even he and his Wellesley Country Club pals could not save them.

"So the guy took up a new cause... Save the Boston Crab. The donor was a wealthy former corporate raider type, turned moonbat.

"The silly urban myth is because he got so many cases of them on Vegas trips that he felt obligated to ensure the crabs' survival, but the reality is that he believed in the overlooked value of the creatures. It's a fact that they do clean the bottom of the water which he envisions will someday boast Trunk Bay clarity.

"We were grateful to Meyer and gave him the senior research analyst position on this project. It meant a lot to the Aquarium and a lotta money came pouring into our coffers from the Prius drivers west of Route 128.

"The only requirement of the position that we forgot to tell Meyer was that he would be doing his research on said crabs from under the Aquarium. And I don't mean with a scuba tank."

"Marl, what the Hell did you to him?" asked Justin as he suddenly understood where this was going.

"Good news, Jus. The crab stocks have returned in record numbers with substantial weight gains and a new sense of vibrance. Suddenly, they took a new liking to hanging around the Aquarium and were somehow being fed. The children are ecstatic when they look down and see very fat, healthy crabs dancing along the bottom in the shallows. Oh, how they cheer with joy! Brings a bittersweet tear to my eye."

Justin could not believe the fate that had befallen his best friend.

"My only complaint, is that I am owed a progress report from Meyer and have not received it in several weeks.

"Shoddy work on the part of your best friend. Does he not understand the meaning of timing deadlines?"

Jus stared with nothing short of fearful bewilderment. He still could not believe that this wasn't a pre-dawn nightmare. Or maybe a Shakespearean ending to one of the playwright's lost tragedies.

"So Jus, we asked question after question about where you might fancy yourself during your sudden retirement."

Jus gazed into the eyes of a wounded serpent. He had indeed entered Medusa's cave. At this moment, the Greek horror figure had nothing on Marlene Dunn.

He was curious as to who the "we" were to whom Marlene was referring.

It turns out that she had the nearest of near-death experiences, and technically found herself on the other side of the proverbial white light for three minutes until being resuscitated. However, unlike many, Marlene did not come back as a grateful and gentler person.

Rather, she returned to this world as a massive amplification of her former self. Her Marshall Stack was turned up to eleven, to the point where the Spinal Tap guys would have blushed.

Kind of like Curious George reborn as King Kong.

Marl took an extended leave from the D.A.'s office, and began to moonlight on her own with some of her former adversaries in the courtroom who got a chuckle out of a partnership with their former nemesis prosecutor. She was dealing in two-bit scrabble jobs, but her legal prowess proved valuable in the contractual theft of items like liquor licenses, taxi medallions, and even a few parking lot expansions for a couple of mobbed-up night clubs.

In the end, her new colleagues really just wanted to get into her pants, however so far to no avail.

Marl had enough of the discussion and looked Justin in the eye, "I know that you're running plates."

Justin was taken by surprise as Marl sneaked up on his guard.

"Are you kidding, Justin? Really? The most talented assassin on the east coast is now living in some two-bit marina in Georgia as a friggin' counterfeiter?"

"Marl," Jus responded. "You cease to amaze me, counselor, but yeah we pick up the phony plates from another vessel halfway between here and Freeport. It's a long haul over open ocean, but our location is totally off the chart, and the margins justify the time and fuel cost. The Bahaman boat meets us halfway and everything is smoothly transacted. We print at a nondescript facility about ten miles west of the bridge. No murder. Nobody gets hurt. Just funny money. The friggin' government does it all day."

Marlene tilted her head and nodded as if genuinely impressed.

Jus continued, "And it's a process. The prints change constantly and we need to stay on top of it, but it's not a violent business and it's damn lucrative. A fresh plate can spit piles of Monopoly money.

"When you think about it, currency is only a perception of value anyway?"

Marlene responded, "Jus, the point is after being technically dead, I refuse to go back to my old life. This time, I want to hold the strings and make the score. No more playing second fiddle to jerk-offs like you. And to be frank, I would dub thee a profound jerk-off.

"You see, I would like to partake in what you have deemed inherently yours. You are correct in that you are talented. You are creative. You supposedly loved me. You lured me to bed. Moreover, you temporarily killed me. You, kind sir, fucking owe me! I feel well entitled to revenge for your heinous deeds, while I'm also curious as to the opportunity that lies here."

Jus motioned for her to pause, "Calm down, Marl. What is it that you want?"

Marlene quickly replied, "Don't interrupt me. I own you. You took my life, temporarily of course, however you have taken my life in a hundred ways.

"I could have you killed this very minute with the subtle sign of asking you to pass the pepper shaker, which is my friend's signal to claim your pathetic soul and hand it over the devil. But that would be too easy. Not worth the plane ticket down.

"My revenge, dear Justin, is going to entail a lot more than just removing you from this blue ball that spins around the sun. I want to take over your world. Your money. Your will. Even your soul, if you pretend to have one. The fucking Christmas Grinch had a bigger heart than you.

"Jus, please understand that I intend to take complete ownership over your very smile. I will own every minute that your cheeks lift up and your ivory-colored teeth greet the world."

Jus interrupted, "Marl. Who is working with you. I can get you a better deal. Who is this bastard with a gun trained on my chest?" hissed a desperate Jus.

"Oh", said Marlene, "My once so perceptive Justin McGee. What makes you so sure your would-be assassin is a man?"

Jus appeared to be genuinely startled.

"You see Justin, with your departure from Boston it did create a bit of a vacuum. And it was an equal-gender opportunity. Her name is Eileen Ulich and she's a fierce German.

"I often wonder if she possesses your acumen behind the rifle scope and against the headboard? However, I would not know, but tonight would be an appropriate time to test her capabilities? That red dot appears to still be steady and consistent."

Little did Justin know, but Marlene's world famous hired gun was really some kid to whom she gave fifty bucks to aim on Justin the most powerful corporate boardroom laser pointer that Amazon inventoried.

"Okay, Marl. I get that you're on medical leave and have faced Hell because of me. I recognized your need for vengeance.

"My guess is that you might be here to perhaps arrest me for plying my new trade. I'm sure that you've shaken your ass around the docks over the past few days under my radar. Trying to learn about me from my rum-soaked dock mates?

"Scenario two, is that you and your new partner are here to get off on taunting me and enjoying the end result of leaving me face down in swamp.

"I see those as your only two avenues. I would honestly have more respect for you if you just chose the latter. So get on with it."

To which Marl responded, "You know, for a smart guy, you'll never get it. Yeah, I served and continue to serve the DA's office with committed pride and all that bullshit. But you know what? Is the pay worth getting my head almost pumpkin-smashed by a puke like you?

"No, my friend. My lover. This time, I hold the trigger. With one phone call, I could have a dozen Feds at this marina in twenty minutes who will toss the joint in search of contraband. If they don't kill you, your dock mates will because we will seize every bit of their drug smuggling grab-bags onboard each of their tubs."

Justin's eyes widened.

"Picture the scene, Justin. All of your rogue marina friends franticly tossing their junk into a burn pile at the end of the dock. What a sight! Just like Savonarola in Florence Square.

"Oh, and I'm sure that none of the boy scouts down here have any priors that we could use against them? Please…

"When word gets back that Tom Baxter, aka Justin McGee, was the biggest hole in the Swiss cheese who brought down the Fed heat, you will make Meyer's fate look like he's right now getting a naked massage and being fed grapes by Jennifer Aniston.

"You will die the slowest of maritime deaths at the hands of your so called mates. At least there will be no shortage of chum bait around here for awhile."

Marl paused and summed up her argument as if in court.

"No, Justin. Regarding your current activities, I possess a clear and different vision. This time, I want in on the operation, and not merely as window dressing, but as your goddamned partner!"

Chapter 2

Georgia Coast (Present Day)

"Dammit!!!"

Michonne Reilly, for the second time tripped on a sky-reaching root and fell face-first into a three inch deep slop of rancid swamp water.

She was firmly resigned to the fact that she would make it. By this point, failure was not an alternative.

For Michonne, to not make it was an unacceptable option.

Moss…

She was so sick of the Georgia swamp moss. The thickness of the humidity gagged her eleven-year old lungs to the point where a pack of Camel no-filters would have felt like an oxygen mask. At random intervals her boots would step in a foot-deep puddle that would immediately engulf her feet in a probing, slimy chill, while the hanging Spanish moss dangled from the trees and softly caressed her cheeks like the touch of a ghost.

Michonne feared that she could hike for years without ever finding fresh water, for the pools around her were the color of motor oil.

Trying to disregard her trepidation, she persevered. Despite her feet screaming wet protest, and the slow onset of dehydration, Michonne moved on.

If one were to meet her on the trail (if there was one), between her naturally mature looks and her tenacity, they easily would have pegged her for three years her senior.

As she crossed over a stream via a fallen tree, she quietly expressed to herself gratitude that the wood was there to provide boot-strap livery.

She made it across only to finally find some solid leaf-covered ground that served as both a swamp clearing and oasis.

At about two o'clock on her Cracker Jack pocket compass, Michonne noticed the small cabin. While it appeared modest, it was rather well-appointed for a desolate swamp. Despite the mold and half-inch layer of dirt enveloping the small house, she took comfort in the pretty curtains and the brightly painted orange and sky blue window boxes.

Michonne approached with stealth. Each step thought out like a move on Bobby Fischer's chessboard. This would be an overly intrepid move for an average little girl, but she was forced to face the world's underbelly at an abnormally young age.

When sneaking up on prey, the only benefit to the mass of fallen swamp leaves were their inherent lack of crunch. In a Georgia swamp, nothing crunched, for years of relentless damp humidity left everything soft and quiet.

Michonne saw Miner Redd sitting in his rocker, albeit there was no movement of his chair.

His snoring was chainsaw loud, but he lacked neither neighbors to complain, nor any local constabulary to deliver their concerns.

He merely slept, snored, and occasionally drooled.

Having no idea that Michonne was watching him in the midst of his humid slumber, he shifted to his right side without skipping a beat of the incessant snoring.

Miner was an ugly sight to behold. The wire-brush hair and crumb filled beard made her cringe. He resembled someone who trick or treated all twelve months of the year.

Yet, she felt no trepidation. She felt no fear. She jettisoned those feelings more and more as her proximately to Miner decreased.

She just stared while trying to understand why she was there as she watched the peacefulness of Miner's afternoon rest, which most likely had begun at around midnight the previous evening.

Michonne got a bit of a chuckle at how his left pant leg was not just stained, but looked like at some point during the night, it opened a sluice for the urine to find its way down and add to the multi-shaded wooden porch stain-work.

She put her foot on the first step, and subsequently leaned her weight forward via her right leg.

"Crack!" was all the stair replied, yet Miner remained in the midst of his wildest dreams.

Step number two. "Snap!" and Miner subtly stirred as he shifted his body weight to his other side.

At that point, Michonne remained quiet and yet surprisingly calm. Fear was not part of her spider web of thoughts, and the more cognitive part of her turned toward logistics.

Last step.

 She proceeded slowly in order to gain access to the main landing of the rickety old cottage.

"Creeeek…"

Suddenly, Miner's left hand shot across the right arm of his chair expecting to swat an insect, yet Jim Beam would not yet release him from his semi-coma lease just yet.

It was then that Michonne removed from her small, child's backpack the scalpel that she had stolen from her recent administering physician's tray when he briefly left the exam room to convey instructions to the nurse. The razor sharp instrument felt and moved so naturally in her hand. It was not unlike the small carving knife which she used to whittle small animal shapes into the large oak log in the Narios' backyard, which was an activity at which she became unusually proficient.

The early morning sunlight caught an angle on the blade, only to momentarily blind her and serve as a mirrorball to shine upon this red-neck dance floor.

Michonne approached Miner slowly, and brought the instrument within three inches of this throat.

Suddenly, he stirred and his arm grabbed Michonne as if he was awake all along and just playing possum. Miner Redd had damned good instincts. Otherwise, he would not have survived this long in his corner of the desolate swamp.

While he wrestled with the little girl's left hand, Michonne managed to slowly, methodically, and borderline artistically, drag the instrument along Miner's flamingo-like gullet, thus relieving him of his pesky Adam's Apple. A spurt of blood shot into her right eye, which she gently wiped away like a baby's tear.

Despite some brief gurgling coming from Miner's throat, the action was swift, calm and quiet.

Michonne stepped back and looked at the results of her work which resembled that of a Kyoto sushi chef. In no way was she in shock or jarred. Rather, she gazed upon Miner's pathetic, lifeless form like a great painter who stares at the completed work on a particularly gratifying canvas.

She remembered back to only a few days ago during the camping trip on which her foster family took her and her so-called brother. Their destination was an RV park in the middle of the wooded Georgia swampland.

Michonne had lived with the Narios for nearly three months when she finally had enough. While her instructors constantly sang her praises to the Narios at all the of the parent/teacher meetings, when the couple actually got around to attending, Michonne still remained a second class citizen within the household.

That's simply because her foster brother was actually the Narios' biological son, who received biological son treatment, while Michonne remained a member of the emotional attention proletariat. She was also the proud recipient of several punishment sessions at the hands of one Marion Nario, when the little girl's attitude and behavior was deemed inappropriate.

Paul Nario had drank himself out of a job as a staff accountant at a large, local hardware and equipment distributor in Savannah, and he and Marion thought how handy it would be to take in some aimless ragamuffin in order to garner a steady monthly check from the State of Georgia. However, Michonne proved to be more of a handful than the Narios expected.

Paul and Marion envisioned a young, waif-like little girl who would quietly mind her business, be polite, go to school and basically shut the hell up when it came to family interpersonal communication.

Much to their chagrin, that was not be the situation.

The first incident occurred when Michonne had only been with the family for a little over a month, when Paul after a day of hot dogs and beer at the Braves game, proceeded to plug up the toilet, which he in turn conveniently instructed young Michonne to grab a plunger and get to work.

She did as instructed, and Paul found said waste contents on the front seat of his Toyota which had been sitting in the scorching southern sun for several hours. Paul was livid, and being the gallant man that he was, called upon his doting Marion to deliver the proper corporal punishment that the incorrigible rogue deserved. Paul was a firm believer that a man never laid a hand on a female, so he justified his sub-contracting of the duties by the fact that they were to be administered by a member of the proper gender. It didn't matter that Marion was twice as tall and had a hundred and ten pounds on Michonne. Paul considered it a fair fight.

Michonne took her beating as she had taken the other ones during the prior weeks. It was a scene without any noise, fuss, or facial expression. She was as stoic as a granite block.

Michonne had been abandoned and orphaned by her meth-head mom around the age of four. Since then, she had been shuffled in and out of facilities from South Carolina to Florida, with Savannah becoming her ultimate destination for the few years prior to being placed with the Narios. By then, after stints in so many varying environments and with so many downright dysfunctional hosts, she was not only seasoned and experienced, but brutally hardened in body, heart and mind.

After enduring a miserable tenure with the Narios and their concept of a kind, generous indentured servitude, the couple announced to Michonne and Paul, Jr. that the family was going to embark on a camping expedition out in the swamps in order to get back to nature and regroup with the love for their ideal environment.

The truth was that Paul, while still out of work, had started a career of selling marijuana to all of their wanna-be yuppie neighbors who were either too scared or too embarrassed to procure it on the street, and who were unable to find any legitimate medical means in which to obtain the herb. Even as legal pot shops were slowly sprouting up around the country, most of residents of the Nario neighborhood would not be caught dead standing in line in front of one, especially with the press now seemingly having a field day with such scenes.

He was due to meet with a contact at the selected campground in order to pick up roughly two pounds of the aromatic plant in hopes of unloading it via the quiet desperation that resided within his little slice of suburbia.

It was from that campground that Michonne escaped only to run into the depraved Miner Redd, and subsequently experience the worst hell on earth that could ever befall a little girl who was already frightened and lost in an apathetic world.

When Miner encountered her, he used a twisted type of fatherly charm to assure Michonne that she would be welcome in his home as a guest to be treated like royalty. What he failed to mention was that while she would be treated like a princess, she would not enjoy the safety of being cloistered in a tower. The only part of Miner that spread out in more wild direction than the hairs on his head, were the two hands that gestured for Michonne each evening.

By fortunate fate, one afternoon during a particularly long drunken stupor-induced nap, she slipped out of the cottage and away from the snoring bastard only to vow to soon return.

Chapter 3

Port Side Vow Marina (Present Day)

Splaasshh!!

As the morning sun blazed a greeting to the new day, Jus and Marlene tussled over who would snag the tennis ball from their neighbor's hooligan-minded golden retriever, Killian. The dog's owner kept his vessel a few slips down from the Free Lance, but the playful pooch often visited with Justin and Marlene when he felt like a little attention or some physical activity.

Killian was not the golden's real name, but for some reason he responded to it at Justin's call. After finding himself living in a marina, and twice voraciously reading John D. MacDonald's twenty-one book Travis McGee series, he felt compelled to pay homage to not only his playful canine friend, but also to his new favorite author. Like the McGee in the MacDonald series, Jus selected a marina as the backdrop for the rest of his life. At least that was the aspiration of the former Boston assassin.

The past several months were a constant ebbing and flowing of tide and memories. While just a couple of years ago, he surrendered to the fact that he was incapable of loving another human being, he now found himself entranced like never before by the likes of the resurrected Marlene Dunn.

A year ago in Boston, shortly after their torrid love affair had commenced, Justin fired a bullet into Marlene's skull from a high-powered rifle from a distant rooftop, only to assume that his track record of fatal accuracy had proven consistent.

Since that horrific day, Marlene proceeded to not only arrive back from the dead at Justin's favorite marina restaurant, but she also confirmed the demise of his best friend and short-lived business partner, Meyer.

While that news pained Jus, he understood the concept of render unto Caesar.

Since Marlene's arrival at Port Side Vow Marina, Jus and she lived together onboard Jus' stately 50-foot Cabo sport-fishing yacht, while successfully running a counterfeit currency operation that was based in Freeport, The Bahamas.

For so many, it would appear to be a profound head-scratcher that Marlene forgave Jus for his most vile sin, but each day while she proceeded with her own greedy agenda, their love rekindled. Their attraction was primal on many levels, as if they existed in a world of their sole command. To them it was a realm where normal customs and rationale did not apply. It was a relationship where even attempted murder could be forgiven, and passion could be rediscovered. They never would expect the outside world to understand, nor did they beg acceptance.

When Jus first fled Boston after the murder attempt, he desperately wanted to retire from the assassin business which was his unorthodox calling for so many years. For him, money was an incentive, but the real motivation remained undiscovered and lurked somewhere within the caverns of his mind.

Events from Justin's past, like the murder of his revered Uncle Rick when Jus was a young boy, fueled his twisted sense of motivation and revenge. Nobody would ever hold his strings or successfully attempt dominion.

While on the run, Justin wanted to flee to neither Mexico nor South Florida, as he found that action step both risky and cliche. Instead, he selected the out of the way, unassuming Port Side Vow Marina in Jekyll Island, Georgia as his ultimate clandestine home.

The hidden boat yard provided a comfortable, semi-hidden slip and a simple, yet quality-fare restaurant. Most importantly, his PSV dock neighbors held firm the coastal tradition of keeping their mouths shut and their eyes closed even under duress from "outsiders", especially anyone that remotely resembled law enforcement.

Justin was certain that most Bostonians had never heard of Jekyll Island, never mind knowing its location. Most likely, the name would only conjure up memories of a creepy line item on a high school English class syllabus, which was precisely the way Jus liked it.

While Jekyll Island seemed a rather esoteric destination, the place held a rich history. The renowned explorer Ponce de Leon served as civil governor during the early 1500s, and the island served as a backdrop for contentious bickering in the years that followed between France, Spain and England as to who had rights to lay claim.

The island eventually evolved into a winter retreat for America's ultra-wealthy in the late 19th Century, until ultimately the state of Georgia acquired the area soon after the end of World War II in an effort to preserve it within its State Park portfolio.

Many of the dockside inhabitants of Port Side Vow were also retired, yet engaged in some not so legal shipping and transportation endeavors. It was the perfect spot if one needed to disappear without concern of being ratted out by those in eyeshot. Justin feared that if he was to hide anywhere inland, he would be surrounded by nosy neighbors who were eager to drop a dime while anticipating a reward purse.

Rows of boats with so many stories of opportunity and various types of escape could be found under the many layers of wood and fiberglass. At Port Side Vow, most captains were running from someone, something or often both.

A few boats away, Captain Stacey Dair had the unique day job of inventory manager for a local cement and cinder block transportation firm. After she figured out how to pull off her scam, she invited her two unemployed cousins, whose resumes and references letters were all authored by Stacey, to apply for jobs as night loaders. Basically, the blocks were stuffed each evening with bags of heroin and cocaine that Stacy hauled earlier in the day aboard her vessel. The contraband was then transported throughout the remainder of the night shift by vehicles which donned the symbol and lettering of an old and well respected local business who was known to engage in normal activity during abnormal hours, thus avoiding suspicion.

When the trucks stopped for a midnight snack at the usual road house, lower level partners with keys to the trucks would quietly relieve the vehicles of their contraband cargo in order to make deliveries. Minutes later, the initial drivers would get back into their rigs and continue on the main roads so the legitimate contents could be delivered in tact before dawn. Everyone was happy and kept their mouths shut. Lucrative under-the-radar scams like Captain Stacey's were quietly operating up and down the rows of docks.

Further down the dock was the vessel Sea-a-torium, whose business model Jus viewed as especially clever. Capt. Billy Tradinski's barge-like boat was marketed as a floating funeral home. Customers who knew that this type of ceremony was usually reserved for the military, would pay to have their deceased loved ones brought aboard with the intention of being buried at sea. After greasing the local licensing officials, on paper Captain Billy held the same credentials required of a funeral director in the state of Georgia.

Only Bill's clients never quite made it to Davy Jone's Locker, as they were far too valuable a commodity when they could be sold to illegal medical and scientific projects. Also, the really fun jobs for Bill involved clients who actually lived to see another day. One of his niche markets was reserved for people who faked their own deaths usually for life insurance scams, but also popular was the client who sought to skip out on alimony payments or a particularly nasty underworld debt.

Captain Bill would take the client's cash, give them a bogus county-sealed death certificate, and host the newly deceased (who was usually joined by a mistress) for a sunset cruise to celebrate his supposed demise. It was the perfect scam and never questioned by anyone at the marina. If anything, most found it amusing. Marlene would sometimes chuckle as she perused the obituaries with a dusk-hour cocktail, only to look over and see the recently departed stagger off of Bill's boat with an empty plastic martini glass and a confetti-tossing bleach blonde.

During the fair-weather periods craved by mariners, the GDP of Port Side Vow exceeded that of several third-world countries. It was fitting that a little known Jekyll Island fact was that in the early 1900s, a group of the nation's wealthiest financiers gathered on the island to discuss monetary policy, which ultimately resulted in the creation of the United States Federal Reserve Bank in 1913.

It was all bitterly ironic considering Justin's newfound island occupation.

Justin noticed that over the past year all of his nautical neighbors went out of their way not to ask questions about one another's affairs - legal or otherwise. It was a symbiotic little corner of the southeast coast which provided total anonymity for those who required such an environment.

Thus, at Port Side Vow, it became a cultural cornerstone not to inquire about a neighbor's endeavors. For instance, if a marina member was having a Sunday cookout, and inadvertently one of the guests on the list was a distant cousin who happened to work for the coast guard or other law enforcement, then the event was immediately canceled due to a spurious emergency or the venue was quickly switched.

In the midst of all of this underground economic and entrepreneurial activity, Marlene landed in Justin's world like that famous German dirigible in New Jersey.

Her attempted assassination was an assignment that Jus would forever regret, but in her twisted way, Marlene now offered forgiveness.

That's not to say that Jus wasn't crestfallen at the news that his lifelong best friend, Meyer, needed to die due to Marlene's distorted idea of weregild. However, Meyer knew the risks that his activity assumed, and Jus was certain that his old friend accepted his fate as a cost of doing business.

At least that's how Jus' icicle heart spoke to him.

Also, his primal attraction to Marlene clouded his rationale. He would often stare at her feminine form like an eight-year old watching the chimney on Christmas Eve.

In an unorthodox synthesis of forgiveness and greed, they forged a very strange chapter-two of their relationship.

"Hey Marl, how are we looking on that shipment for Thursday night?"

To which Marl responded, "We're okay, babe. Looks like we have a half dozen plates coming in with new issues of twenties and fifties. Should be a strong printing if we can get Gerbil to get the friggin' ink hue right this time."

"I know, I know…" responded Justin with a half-wave at the air, "We gotta stay on him about paying attention to detail. Jus was not taking the risk lightly, but he now played in a different arena. During his tenure as a Boston assassin, he alone controlled all aspects of the operation. Now, the rules were different and all of the moving parts forced him to abandon his firm notion of being king of all he surveyed.

"This should be a nice haul, Marl. Hey, while we're just hanging out playing with Killian, I need to broach a subject."

Marl began to look more intently.

"Look, we have a good situation here. To have you back in my life is the ultimate gift. However, we can't just print dummy money forever. We need to consider our future. Counterfeiting has been good to us, but like any project, the longer that we engage, the more risk we take of getting pinched.

"Our delivery contacts in Freeport have been badgering me about taking on another business line. You know, increasing the scope of our activity. I mean, we have the distribution means in place, but maybe our product portfolio needs a little diversification?"

That garnered Marl's attention. "Another business line, Jus? What pray-tell cockamamie scheme do you have in mind this time, Captain?"

Jus paused and looked Marlene in the eyes and simply replied, "People."

Marl was quiet and failed to immediately figure out how to respond,

"People? What do you mean by people?

"Are you suggesting that we start importing Bahaman girls to serve as sex slaves or some other kinky shit? Has all of this salt air rotted out your damned cerebrum?" challenged a startled Marlene.

"Not even close," responded Jus. "I'm suggesting that we drink from a cup that is already being poured. Sweets, the Bahaman Islands are becoming a crossroads for illegal immigrants arriving from Eastern Europe and Africa. They stop there to get their shit together and gather their bearings and bogus documents. Then, they figure out a way to sneak into the States via some dope smuggler or fishing boat who's pounding sand during a slow streak.

"Think of it. They're gonna get here somehow regardless of what the TV tells you, so why not provide the livery service? Honey, we could make a killing."

Marlene paused and then proceeded, "So, Captain Einstein, you're telling me that we're going to start importing friggin' people, not pieces of metal, and sneak them onto the coast only to further the immigration overrun in this country? Wow, what a patriot…"

"Marl, they're comin' anyway, whether it's on the Queen Mary or a friggin inner tube. All I'm saying is that we can make a buck as an intermediary for a process that is already well in place and will thrive with or without us."

Immersed in thought for several seconds, Marl stared at the horizon.

"Jus, when you say that we can make money, how much are you talking? Is this an endeavor even worth pursuing? All we need is the damn Coast Guard to board us or some other Homeland Security shit to take a liking to our boat. I just don't see how it's worth it."

"Marl, we're talking a going market rate of four thousand per head just to bring them to the mainland from the half-way point between here and Grand Bahama. It's the same damn trip that we take to get the plates, only these plates walk, talk and possess a higher level of danger while transporting. Say we can fit twenty of 'em down below? Immediately, we have ourselves a profitable charter. We'd need to bring Gerbil along for security and pay him a flat rate. But even after factoring in his services and of course then fuel cost, for eighty grand, we're still netting out a noble score. Think of the lemmings to our west. Most of 'em, after paying the silly tax man, need to work a whole year to take down less what we could do in two days!"

Justin's continued pitch slowly started to tickle Marlene's fancy.

"I dunno, Jus. Let me mull it over. At first glance, this proposition is insane."

"But?" Jus shot back.

It was at that moment that Jus and Marl noticed out of the corners of their eyes a little girl staggering down the dock.

They were in shock, for it was a rarity to see a child at Port Side Vow, never mind one who looked like Lil' Orphan Annie on a crack-bender.

The young girl approached the couple in a completely disheveled manner, yet with a gait that exuded no apparent fear.

"Please. Do you have any water?" asked an exhausted and dehydrated Michonne Reilly.

Marl and Jus stared in shock at what they were witnessing. The poor kid looked like she had just spent a month in a dryer's spin cycle, only to be then rolled in the peat moss.

Marl processed what she was seeing and responded, "Stay here, dear. I'll be right back."

Jus just continued to stare at this poor soul.

Marl returned quickly with a cold bottle of spring water.

Michonne eagerly grabbed it and began chugging the cool water, which caused her to cough and choke.

"Little sips, sweety." coached Marlene.

After a moment, Marl grabbed a deck chair and softly convinced Michonne to sit down and rest.

"What's your name honey? How old are you?" asked Marl.

The little girl coughed twice and replied, "My name's Michonne. Michonne Reilly and I'm eleven years old. I think?"

"Wow, that's such a pretty name, and eleven years old means you're a big girl. Honey, how did you get here? You look like you've been out in the woods or some swamp."

Michonne Reilly? thought Justin. The Bostonian didn't see a bit of Irish in the little girl's visage. Rather, she resembled the daughter of a former law partner whose family was from Central America.

"I was in the swamp," replied Michonne after semi-choking on a gulp. "I had to go visit a man. He was a very bad man."

Marl handed the girl a napkin and asked, "Well, that was kind of you to go visit him. I'm sure he was happy to see you. But that's not nice if he was a bad man. Why was he a bad man, dear? You can tell me."

Michonne paused for several seconds while sipping more water, "He did very mean things to me and touched me and…" The little girl's face cringed as if about to weep.

Marl tried to console her, "It's okay Michonne. Some people do bad things to very nice little girls. Honey, why did you go see this man if he was mean? And what happened while you were visiting him?"

Michonne responded in her subtle Southern drawl, "I kilt him. I kilt him real good."

Marl met eyes with Jus, and then turned back to Michonne, "Honey, if you say that you hurt this bad man, what did you do to him?"

She was quiet and drank from the bottle, then winced and continued.

"I was at the doctor's office after the man did very bad things to me, and the doctor had some kind of knife that I stole. I kilt the bad man with that little knife."

Jus and Marl were both transfixed with shock at hearing Michonne's story.

Marlene looked at Justin and stepped back, "Listen dear, you need to get cleaned up. I'm gonna get you some soap and shampoo, and you can borrow my robe so you can take a nice, hot shower. I'll be right back."

Jus gently patted the girls matted hair, "Here, just sit and relax. Sounds like the bad man is gone and you look exhausted."

Marl quickly returned and directed Michonne to where the marina showers were. She made sure that the girl was comfortable and returned down to the dock to Jus.

"Jus, what the hell did we just hear?"

"I dunno, Marl. She's a little kid - maybe a runaway? Could be just be a fantasy story. Something maybe she saw on Law & Order or some other shit?"

"I don't think so, Jus. Did you see those eyes go absolutely ablaze as she told that tale? No way did she make that up."

"Marl. This is way above our pay grade. We gotta call DSS or the Sheriff's Office or something."

"Jus! If she's telling the truth and they find that dead diddler, then she'll end up in a juvenile detention center or mental institution for the rest of her life. We can't do that to her! You know I had a fucked up childhood that was not my fault. Should I have been sent away?"

Jus looked up and blew the hair from his eyes while remaining quiet.

Marl looked around, "Moreover, I don't think that we can afford to have law enforcement stomping around these docks. Last time I checked, there were still a few Boston FBI units looking for your ass! And I'm not too sure that our neighbors would care for our inviting such guests. Can't we just let her stay with us for a bit until we can figure this shit out? I can shoot into town and get her fresh clothes and a toothbrush. It's not like we don't have the room on your damn yacht."

"Marl, are you insane? Are you proposing that we semi-adopt this kid? We know nothing about her, or how to care for a young girl. We can barely take care of us! What if she loses it and decides to go scalpel on you and I at two in the morning?"

"Jus. We're being kind to her. She was obviously molested and most likely in a state of shock. I think we're safe. C'mon. Just temporarily through the weekend. We'll make a decision on what to do with her on Monday."

Jus slowly shook his head. He had a high tolerance and patience with Marlene, for he had after all tried to kill her once. He often cut her slack even though it was against his gut intuition, something which usually dominated the longtime assassin's thought process.

"Alright Marl," exhaled Jus, "Go get her some clothes and I'll make sure she's okay to bring aboard the boat. Maybe I can get her to rest in the guest state room. The starboard one has the big bed and is more comfortable than the drunk bunks across the hall."

Marl smiled and kissed Jus on the cheek.

"Thank you, Captain," Marl winked and walked quickly down the dock and up the gangway.

Chapter 4

Home of Gerbil Turner

Gerbil Turner was a proverbial pain the ass. Marlene especially couldn't stand him, but she tolerated his antics during operations. Despite an eight-year old's mentality, most times Gerbil proved to be an effective business partner. If given the right set of plates, he could crank out bogus currency that could fool the Secretary of the Treasury.

He also proved valuable when it came to the required extra security needed for high-risk assignments.

At six-foot four, two hundred and thirty pounds, the former Georgia State linebacker commanded an intimidating presence, not to mention that he was a master with automatic weapons, and really with any kind of violence that was required during a job.

The only thing that Gerbil loved more than making money and cracking skulls, was the company of prostitutes of the non-Caucasian persuasion. He was no racist in that he loved to fornicate with Asians, African Americans, Muslims, you name it. Just no white chicks. Justin always found this strange, yet Marl speculated that earlier he life he was most likely berated or abused by either a Caucasian teacher or babysitter, and that he took it out on all white girls who ultimately lost their appeal. He was the purist of rednecks, and was most proud of his scratchy old vinyl country/western record collection and his adoration for cheap, warm beer. Merle Haggard was a god, and Elvis, albeit appeared a little fruity to Gerb, sat at ol' Merle's right hand.

At the moment he was eagerly awaiting the arrival of some new plates from Jus and Marlene so that he could quickly begin the work that he did best. Gerbil was certainly more of a leg-breaker than an atom-splitter, and it remained a marvel that he could enjoy such a high level of success at his craft. However, he was gifted as a young man with the unique job opportunity of working for a counterfeiter while eking his way through school, and had learned the skill by concentrating with a curious eye.

When Gerbil was on, he was the best, but he could be sloppy and at times compromised important shipments. However, like a major league power hitter, if he could smash the ball only a third of the time, he still might be bound for Cooperstown. Thus, Jus and Marlene tolerated his shenanigans.

They appreciated his role as operational muscle during high-risk runs, and they got a kick out of Gerb's sense of creativity when it came time to applying the clamps.

Recently, a shipment of plates was on its way up from Freeport to rendezvous mid-way with Free Lance, when the Bahaman transport crewmen were pirated by some two-bit dope jockeys who fancied themselves as players. While Jus, Marl and Gerb were en route, they were alerted of the robbery, and were told of the pirate vessel's course. The Free Lance eventually caught up with the boat in question in order to retrieve their intended shipment. While Marlene aimed her Glock at one of the scoundrels, Gerbil boarded the absconders' 32-ft. Regulator, and immediately put the captain in a boa constrictor-strength head lock.

Where he always enjoyed impressing Jus and Marl, he decided to get creative.

Gerbil raised one of the pirates' outboard engines out of the water and fired it up in gear. He needed to act fast, for the impeller would soon burn out by being out of the water. He quickly thrust the captain over the top of the roaring motor.

The first-mate pleaded, "Why are you doing this? We've not hurt you! Take your shit! Let us go! We'll never steal again! PLEASE!"

Gerbil chuckled and shot back, "True. You'll never steal again!"

Gerbil then lowered the skipper onto the spinning propeller.

The pirate not only shrieked an inhuman holler, but shook like Candlestick Park during the World Series Quake. San Fran registered a 6.9 magnitude on the Richter Scale that day, where this guy was sporting a solid 10.

Gerb's only regret was that the fun had ended too soon, for the outboard blew out fast from overheating.

At any rate, Gerbil took a look at what was left of the captain and tossed him overboard as some alms to the Bull Sharks.

As Gerbil watched the blood slick being formed by the out-going tide, his mind wandered back to when he was in his late teens. He was out on a day of joy cruising in his shit-kicked Mustang that looked like it went through an acid car wash.

Along for the ride was Buffy Johansen, who had been forbid-den by her family to associate with the likes of Gerbil Turner, which made him all the more irresistible to the privileged Southern Belle. As cargo, he brought along a bottle of rot-gut bourbon that he snagged at the local Fuel & Suds, where as usual, Gerb procured three dollars worth of watery gas and five dollars worth of sandpaper for the throat.

The giddy couple cruised along the Georgia countryside when suddenly Gerb heard a siren and immediately saw blue lights invading his rear-view mirror.

He pulled over to the side of the road almost effortlessly, for the junker's bent axle inherently veered the car to the right.

As the officer approached the sad excuse for a vehicle, Gerbil capped the bottle and tossed the booze in the backseat. The "clink" from hitting two other empty bottles was so loud that the trooper could not help but realize that this was going to be a layup of an arrest.

"License and regist... Hey asshole, you know the drill. Just give me your damn papers!"

Buffy merely cowered in silence and curled in the passenger's seat, while Gerbil feverishly fished through his coverless glovebox.

"Officer, it seems in all of my absent-mindedness, I must have left my papers back at the ranch. Silly me with so much on my mind these days. But I did bring my wallet, so maybe we could find a way to settle things nice and easy right here?"

"Outta the car d-bag, and keep your hands where I can see them!"

With that Gerb slowly opened the jalopy's door, got out and leaned against the hood. The officer patted him down and muttered, "Sit tight," and spoke into his radio in garbled tones.

When the officer was finished he said to Buffy, "Juliet, I need to take Romeo for a ride to the station. I just called another officer who will be along in two minutes to bring you home. Y'all have a nice day now."

The trooper led a half-smirking Gerbil to the backseat of the squad car and drove away leaving Buffy behind whose eyes began to drip with tears.

Back at the county police station, Gerb was forced to don foot shackles and hip-side handcuffs. He and the arresting officer looked like Montressor and Fortunato as Gerb was led down a dark and damp hallway.

The trooper opened the cell and shoved his guest inside while placing his foot in front of Gerb's shin so that he did a complete face plant on the dirt-ridden cement floor. While blood began to seep out of Gerbil's nose, he looked up and saw the Hockmeyer twins who were well known in the county, not only because of their incessant run-ins with the local constabulary, but also because they both bore a stark resemblance to Cooter from *The Dukes of Hazzard*. Their necks were such a unique shade of red, that they could have licensed their own Crayola color.

"Well, if it isn't Ol' Gerbil from up-county," quipped Snake Hockmeyer.

To which his brother Caw replied, "Well, I'll be dipped in shit. It sho' look like him. Hey Snake, ain't this the fellah that stoled dat nice gin still we had in the shed? The one that we sure loved and cherished like a baby in a basket. Now Gerbil, we can understand why you might want to borrow our prop'ty for an afternoon, however that was last 'yar and I ain't seen it yet rightly returned."

He turned to his brother, "Hey Snake, that ain't right neighborly, is it?"

Snake responded, "No, sho' isn't. Mr. Gerb, it appears to us that you might owe us a bit of shall we call it, rent. I mean, it only seems fair."

Caw smiled and nodded as Snake continued, "See here, you should know that in this part of the state after a few days, borrowin' equals stealin'. And down here neighbors don't steal from neighbors, 'specially other good, God fearing, community-minded folks."

Now Gerbil was by no means a small guy and could certainly handle himself. But at that age he had not yet grown into the certifiably insane adult into which he would eventually evolve. At this stage, he was no match for these two evolutionary step-skippers.

Snake stared at a now heavily-perspiring Gerbil, "I think that this severe violation on your part calls for an equal violation on our part. Look at me, boy!

"Caw, y'all bring any bandage?"

"Nah, but the way I see it Snake is when we're done, we can just wrap him up in that there toilet paper."

And for the next ten minutes, the two back-swamp cretins took turns banging away at Gerb's head and body. As he lay face first on the filthy floor, blood continued to heavily flow from his nose. The crimson pool was diluted only by a stream of tears. All that could be heard by the officers down the hall was the rattling of Gerbil's shackles against the cement, and the primal grunts of two very amused Georgia pig farmers. The guards snickered as they envisioned that smart ass Gerbil being treated like a rabid swine, and all they did was smile.

"Caw, y'all got any WD-40 or somethin?" asked a crook-ed-grinning Snake.

"Naw, man, but I got myself some purty good spit built up in my mouth from this here chaw I'm workin."

Snake grunted, "Reckin' that'll do."

The last sounds that Gerbil heard before unconsciousness seized him were the thud of two shit-kicker boots being tossed against the wall, and the quick unzip scream from Snake's faded jean fly.

"The way I see it right about now boy, is yo' ass is an Osaka shoe factory," snickered Snake, "And I'm Godzilla…"

Fast-forward to present day.

Impatiently, Gerbil continued to wait to hear from Jus and Marl. While biding his time, he decided to call one of his favorite service professionals.

When Lu picked up the phone, Gerbil so eloquently said in a butchered Asian accent, "Lu-Lu, me so horny…"

He was quite the class act, and not familiar with Stanley Kubrick.

Gerbil loved to tell Lu-Lu funny stories. One of his favorites was about the time when his eyes were starting to fail and that he feared that he might be going blind.

He went on to say that he met with a particularly attractive ophthalmologist and requested that she perform an immediate examination.

Gerb told her in distress, "I'm goin' blind, doc!"

The doctor began the process, but after a minute stepped back and said to Gerbil, "Um... I think you need to stop masturbating."

Gerb responded, "Whaddya mean? That's why I'm goin' blind?"

In frustration, the doctor's shoulders dropped with a quick exhale and replied, "No, dummy. I'm trying to give you an eye exam. Now, knock that off!"

Lu-Lu rolled her eyes while feigning a chuckle and the usual price was negotiated. With the date set for that evening, Gerbil began to wait in anticipation.

Chapter 5
Port Side Vow Marina

As Michonne quietly caught up on some sleep aboard Free Lance, Justin sat Marlene down and poured her a much needed glass of Pinot Grigio.

Marl was worried sick about this little girl, as her once non-existent maternal instincts were suddenly kicking in.

However, Jus had business to discuss.

"Marl, I know you're concerned about her, but just let her rest and we can decide what to do later.

"Right now we need to discuss Shark's offer for the transportation work."

Marl shot back, "You mean how we're going to start human trafficking, Justin?"

Jus was polite as he ignored her comment.

"Like I said, it's about four thousand dollars per head, per trip. We can make some serious money in a short time, but we have to decide as I need to get back to Shark. He's getting antsy, and while he's generous to give us right of first refusal, the clock is running and the business will quickly go elsewhere. Shark is a friend and all, but in the end, like most people all he really cares about is sex and money, and not necessarily in that order.

"The good thing is that he himself is considering some other piece of work that is all hush, hush and he needs to head down

45

to Miami which buys us some time. However, we gotta either commit or lose what in my mind is a great opportunity."

Marl, while both exhausted and concerned, was flirting with that part of her inner self that was usually reserved for a Boston courtroom, but still reared its fiery head even in a quiet barrier island marina.

"Jus, it just seems so damned risky. We gotta good thing going here just printing Monopoly money. If we start bringing illegals aboard the Free Lance, then the human element kicks in. What the fuck happens if these damned Nigerians or wherever the hell they're from, adopt a fondness for our vessel and figure they'd just assume have it for themselves. We've endured a lot, but a mutiny is not yet on our training resume. You know? They take over the damned boat, slit our throats and feed us to the Barracudas."

"Marl. That's why we have Gerbil and his automatic weapons. He will have an AK-47 pointed at all of them for the entire duration of the damned trip. If one of them twitches the wrong way, he'll be instructed to give the guy's head the old Swiss cheese. We get our eighty grand up front, so who cares? Whoever gets out of line ends up in the drink with nobody the wiser. That body won't float in these waters for more than five minutes before the sharks move in and make it a memory. Or better yet, we'll just wrap the prick up in anchor chain and let him sink like a stone for crab food."

Marl was shocked, "Wow, Jus! Now, you're raising the stakes on our whole operation. So, we just what, stop dealing in plates and start running some murderous version of the fuckin' Mayflower? I don't like it, Jus. Don't like it at all."

Jus responded, "Marl, we have a good thing going with the counterfeiting, but it's a dying business. It's not going to be here in five years. Maybe three? The government is getting too wise, and the technology is becoming too sophisticated when it comes to sniffing out bad bills. With human trafficking, there will never be a shortage of clients as long as our soft belly country keeps doling out free-bees to anyone who can fog a mirror."

Jus paused as he noticed the look of inevitable capitulation on Marlene's face.

"Plus, Marl. We have an advantage in that Uncle Sam's defense line is focused on places like Southern Florida and Texas. How many immigration officers do you think that there are in friggin Georgia? I guarantee that you're not going to swing a cat and hit one. We'll be real quiet and totally under the radar. We'll dump the people off a little further up the coast and let them figure it all out. Once they hit land, it's not our problem. We did our part fair and square. It's a great gig, babe."

Marlene took a deep breath as she leaned back. Jus could not resist being taken by the glistening shine of her sun-brown, tight midriff. The firmness of her breasts forced a slow, deep breath from Jus, as he inhaled the smells and sounds of the sea.

She noticed a change in his look and the angle of his glance.

"I dunno, sailor boy. Not sure what you're getting into this time."

Jus snickered.

"Hopefully, it might just be you," he said with a bawdy smirk as he slowly reached over and began to rub her right shoulder while his other hand finger-danced on the small of her back.

"Justin, no. Not now. The little girl is sleeping."

"Yes, indeed she sleeps, my dear. By the look of her, she's gonna sleep 'til Tuesday. That's probably the most comfortable bed that she's slept on in years."

Their mouths met in a tender kiss as Jus helped his lover to her feet. They walked hand in hand onto the boat, and after quickly checking on Michonne, Jus quietly shut and locked the main stateroom door behind them.

He turned and met her full embrace. It took mere seconds for Marlene to abandon her swim clothes and pull off Jus' shirt. They fell onto the bed in silence, partly so they would not awaken their guest, but more because their stares were sparking a fire that yearned to blaze.

He swam slowly into her beckon, and entered while being welcomed by her eager inhale.

Chapter 6
Aboard the vessel Booty Call

Captain Shark Bertolami piloted his 40-foot Hatteras Sportfish while slowing into the opening that allowed the cruel Atlantic to court the calm waters behind the strip of land just north of Miami known as Bal Harbour, Florida.

He was about as close to a modern day pirate as one could envision, and named his vessel Booty Call not only as a payment of homage, but also to offer tribute to other ancillary activities. While he did not sport Johnny Depp scarves and braids, he most certainly carried the swagger and attitude. Quick with both his tongue and fists, Shark was not to be taken lightly, especially in open water out of eye and ear shot of marine authorities.

With a salt-hardened face and an attitude to match, he was the Neptune of all he surveyed. Woe to the seafarer who would occasionally mistake Shark's high-tide colored deep blue eyes as a sign of serenity or possible old English quarter, if crossed.

Shark lived an unorthodox lifestyle in the minds of most, but he made his own rules and never answered to anyone. Or never did for long.

While upon first look at the career sea dog, one may have viewed him as a bit of a rogue. However, he was as competent a captain as any seasoned coast guardsman, and was as hungry with his business dealings as any Wall Street self-important hotshot. Not necessarily evil or depraved, but Captain Shark's demeanor was merely a product of his Darwinian lifestyle.

At the moment, he was running late for a meeting with a potential new client at the lobby bar at the famed OceanView Hotel.

Shark's first mate, Peeler, got the lines ready in order to make the vessel fast to the temporary dock space. With a long, drawn facial structure and particularly high cheekbones, Peeler resembled Cinderella's original wicked witch. Skinny to the point of looking malnourished, Shark would often tease him on the sidewalk about being careful not to fall through the sewer grates. His long stringy Chris Robinson hair, while not conducive to life in the hot sun, was convenient every October 31st.

Peel adeptly secured the lines and shot a quick "Dog, stay!" look at the Booty Call. Shark cut the engines, killed the blower and took a deep breath. From a contact in Bimini, this was promised to be an interesting meeting full of potential opportunity, and supposedly for the parties in play, Shark's name was at the top of the list of captains to hire for the operation. He had no idea what was the scope of the work, but he knew his contact in Bimini, and realized that it must be serious enough if he was being encouraged to travel the lengthy distance to Southern Florida to hear the proposal first-hand.

He and Peeler hopped onto the dock and proceeded to walk the short distance to the historic hotel. As they strolled, Shark could not only smell the salt air, but he also sensed a stronger fragrance which was one of opportunity in the form of quick cash.

Chapter 7
Home of Gerbil Turner

Gerbil's sweat covered body slid off Lu Lu's tiny frame.

He was exhausted but felt quite satisfied not only in the physical sense, but also because he felt that he received his money's worth.

Gerb was a great coupon-cutter.

He slowly turned toward Lu Lu and began gently twirling her thin, raven, sweat-soaked hair. Rubbing her chest she grimaced when realizing that it was not her sweat. She kept the aestheticians busy at the salon, for her molasses colored eyes were always highlighted by perfectly trimmed eyebrows and lashes. She had a smile that could light a candle, and a certain innocence about her that many unfortunate souls often mistook for a dim sense of intelligence. Intentionally, she masked her intellect by an Oscar winning performance of the role of a mental lightweight. It was this personality angle that made her invaluable to business partners in the art of obtaining sought-after information.

She looked him in the eyes and said, "Mr. Turner, that was wonderful. It is so nice of you to spend time with me when you're always so busy running around. I don't really know why you're so busy all the time, because it's not clear what you do for a living. You don't exactly seem to punch a clock, but you're always on the move."

Gerbil in the post-coitus euphoria and warm-down responded, "I'm an entrepreneur, honey. That's all you need to know."

Lu got up and went into the other room, only to return a few minutes later with two slightly steaming cups of tea. She handed one to Gerb, who immediately shrugged it off, and reached for the one that she held for herself. Despite viewing Lu-Lu as harmless, Gerbil didn't take any chances.

"Drink it, Mr. Turner. It's good for you. It's all natural."

"All natural," snickered Gerb, "Great. So's shit, piss and puke."

Lu-Lu had learned to ignore Gerbil's crassness, especially when she was on the hunt for information, and at this moment her curiosity was simmering and approaching a boil.

"So, you can't tell me anything about your work? You're such an intriguing man. I bet your stories are interesting."

This is where it got dicey. Conventional wisdom holds that the local tavern is the most dangerous place where to open one's mouth. However, the pub pales in comparison to the perils of moving the jaw across a soft pillow shared by an eager siren.

Gerbil now felt that he had to prove his manhood, and his mojo immediately kicked in.

"Well Lu, I'm an artist and I like to make things. You know. I'm the creative type."

To which wide-eyed Lu responded, "Mr. Turner, if you're an artist, why do I not see any paintings?"

Gerbil thought about his response, but traded prudence for boasting, "That, baby doll, is why my art is different. My craft is unique, and unfortunately I cannot exactly display it upon my walls. What I create is special and cannot be done by many others. I take a lot of pride in that and it affords me a nice living."

Lu-Lu's cranial wheels spun faster, "Well Mr. Turner, what do you create? I'm interested. All I know about artists is that they paint and draw pretty pictures."

What came next is why Gerbil was a danger to any operation.

"You see, sweet pants, I paint money."

Lu replied, "How does anyone paint money? I don't understand. That makes no sense. Money is already painted green."

Gerbil just couldn't keep his mouth shut.

"Lu, we don't just paint the money for fun. We create it. We make our own fake money so that we can then trade it for real money and everyone is happy. I do it right here in my shop. I have partners down at Port Side Vow Marina who run half-way to Grand Bahama to get the plates, then bring 'em back here so I can practice my art. It's magic. And we're making a lot of money doing it."

And so it was then that the idiot known as Gerbil Turner could not know what he had just set in motion with the Georgia Coast's version of a Shakespearean fool.

Chapter 8

Bar at the OceanView Hotel, Bal Harbour, FL

Shark and Peeler entered the OceanView bar, and were greeted with the same eyes that would welcome two Klan members to a show at the Apollo.

They were met by an austere maître d' who gave them a look as if to ask them if they were lost.

"Gentlemen, may I help you?" he asked them as if just having swallowed vinegar.

Shark responded, "We're here for a three o'clock appointment, and to be frank, I'm not even sure who we're meeting with."

"Hmm," responded the wary snob, "Well, perhaps I can seat you at the bar while you wait in comfort with one of our famous martinis?"

"I don't drink," said Shark, "And trust me Governor, you don't want me starting back up here and now."

"I see," said the host in a tone mixed with contempt and a dash of fear, "Please allow me to show you to a comfortable table."

Shark and Peeler were led to a corner high-top that overlooked the aqua-sheened Atlantic.

Shark tried to make himself comfortable, but it was impossible at that point. He ordered a ginger ale with a dash of cranberry, while Peeler selected a locally brewed pale ale.

Peeler asked, "Skip, what the hell is this all about? Ya know, all this cloak and dagger shit. What kind of gig is this?"

"I dunno know, Peel. Hopefully we'll figure it out soon, or we're getting back aboard the Call and getting the hell out of this snobatorium. We belong here like Rosie O'Donnell at a track meet."

The two were quiet. Unusually quiet. To be the one without the lay of the land was not Shark's customary role. He was used to being in command and calling the shots from the helm.

Shark's determined and focused mind began to wander, and he found himself drifting off to memories as he often did while trying to concentrate.

Shark was fourteen years old when his much older Cousin Bridge asked Shark's dad if he would let his son work on Bridge's fishing boat, Remora, as a deck-hand for the summer.

Shark's dad, who was a well known east coast yacht broker, placed Shark in the hands of his cousin and offered encouragement.

Shark was thrilled. The job meant that he would have to relocate to The Hamptons for the summer, but he viewed that as more an enticement than an inconvenience.

The first time in his life when he felt important was when his cousin assigned to him the illustrious task of "bait boy" underneath the bridge that spanned Shinnecock Bay.

Shark would rip chunk after chunk with his reeking bare hands with the fervor of a seventeen year old picking up his junior prom date.

Snapping out of his daydream and returning to the present, Shark asked his mate, "Hey Peeler. When was the first time in your life you felt important?"

Peeler paused and replied, "I dunno boss. Actually never did, I guess."

With his hunch confirmed, Shark returned to his childhood memory...

After a long day of fishing, Cousin Bridge's crew had enough of the pounding sun and agreed to call it a trip.

Bridge turned to Shark. "Hey kid, we gotta get back. Can you slop up all of this shit? Damn stripers are listless today 'cause of the heat."

At that age, Shark would have heeded his cousin's order to charge unarmed into a no-man's land in the French countryside.

"Aye, aye, Captain Bridge. No problem."

Shark sensed a slight change in Cousin Bridge's voice, but shrugged it off.

Cousin Bridge took the helm and slowly cruised the boat westward back to his home port at Aldrich Marina.

"Guys, sorry the fish were sleepin'. Oh well, the beer was cold. You guys want another for ride home?"

Bridge turned to his nephew, "Hey Gunga Din, more water!"

The captain cleared his throat, "As you know, the reason that we're here is to honor our fallen brother, Peach Malone. They're wakin' him tonight in Riverhead. Hopefully, you'll stay in Quogue as my guests, so we can go together and bid him a proper farewell."

Bridge paused, while the group grunted and nodded.

"With that said, we have to discuss one piece of business that Peach left behind. It concerns quite a bit of money that will be conveniently left out of the probate proceedings.

"You guys remember that score that we nailed down in Florida, near Pompano? Well, it seems that Peach forgot to remember his partners upon his untimely passing, and we can't seem to find the proceeds."

"Uh-oh," said one of the crew, "Not sure we're gonna like the end of this story."

Bridge sipped his beer and continued, "The grieving widow, Madame Peach, seems to have experienced a lapse in memory during her period of sorrow. She's playing that whole damsel in mourning routine."

Shark listened carefully as he tried to figure out what this was all about.

Bridge continued, "Anyway, those land-lease deals that we were supposedly getting from Peach in exchange for cash and access to product distribution, wound up a one-way transaction.

"Peach got a heavy suitcase, but it appears that Madame has decided to keep the lease deals for herself.

"Romantic. A loving inheritance, I suppose. Most wives I know just get a fuckin' IRA payout and an outstanding bookie tab."

Young Shark at this moment was transfixed. Even at such a tadpole age, he realized that this was important. Very important.

Bridge continued to address his colleagues.

"You see, Madame Peach possesses what we negotiated with hubby. She did not earn it. She never loved Peach, as she was banging half of the cabana boys in Delray."

Bridge's colleagues stared at him in disbelief. They had been screwed by a dead man. None of them were especially proud of their drug trade activity, but the return on investment had been lucrative over the years.

Like any business transaction where the capital investment is speculative at best, a few wondered out loud, "Shit, Bridge. How do we get it back?"

Bridge continued, "You see, the exact cause of the dearly departed's demise still remains a secret. The police reports are inconclusive, and he left everything to his old lady. Our business with Peach was of course, never recorded, and there are no probate filings in our world. Thus, in the eyes of the law, she gets everything.

"I talked to our friends in Havana, and their estate settlement system is a bit different. In their wisdom, they realize the value of partners with earning potential which exceeds that of Madame Peach.

"We as a consortium stand to realize an amazing opportunity going forward. I know through Ricky Roach, in Miami, that Peach's wife is already laying the bricks that will build her supposed distribution network. Normally, I would admire her level of industriousness, however in this case, her noble level of drive is at our expense, gentlemen."

Micky McStein, one of the Bridge's right hand men, immediately caught where this was going.

"So boss, you're telling us that this chick's sense of entitlement is the only thing standing in the way of not only our recouping our investment with Peach, but also with any of those plump future scores?"

To which Bridge replied, "Steiny, it's as clear as Cristal bubbly. However, we gotta be careful. To Madame's credit, she's got a lotta eyes. Now, I'm sure that we all agree that a proper settlement must be smoothly negotiated, and I mean like, today.

"I'm convinced that over time Madame Peach will not want to play in our dirty sandbox. She's never seen the messy end of a bait slick, and I'm confident that when reasoned with, she'll just want a fair pay-out to just go away. Of course, we'll have her pledge a solemn oath that she not write some fuckin' book or go blabbing to the FBI, lest her retirement will last a matter of hours and not decades, as planned."

To which the group all laughed. They felt relieved, for they wanted their lease deals, but in no way did the group seek to murder a widow.

Bridge continued, "Guys, let's get home and shower up. We'll go to the wake like gentlemen and pay our respects to our former partner. Let's support the widow in her time of sorrow, as she will hopefully honor her husband's wishes and vision."

Shark could not believe what he was hearing. All he wanted to do was cut bait and scrub the boat to please his cousin.

Hours later, after the gang cleaned up and had donned proper calling hours suits, they arrived at the funeral home still reeking of herring oil.

As usual, Bridge led the group while the others followed with young Shark playing the role of caboose.

The service was not exactly standing room only, as Peach's business activities did not support an environment that included actual friends.

Cousin Bridge motioned for the group to go ahead.

"Hey, fellahs. You guys g'won up ahead. I'll be right there, and ah, tell the kid to stay with me."

"Sure, boss," replied a curious McStein.

The mood was solemn, yet not a tear was being shed.

While somewhat liked and tolerated, Peach was a conniving bastard while he was vertical. Bridge chuckled to himself at the vision of the deceased up in the clouds counting his money. If there was anyone who could have taken it with him, it was Peach Malone.

As the gang moved through the feeble semblance of a line, Bridge politely hugged, kissed and expressed condolences to Madame Peach.

Shark had never been to a wake, but he found it odd that there were two rough looking guys at the door carefully watching everyone who entered, and who actually frisked Bridge and his crew. Apparently, the grieving widow was on high alert.

Shark took in the moment, then suddenly felt the need to stay close to his cousin.

When Bridge finally reached the widow in line, he gave her the archetypal half-hug and an unconvincing, "Madame, I'm so sorry for your loss. I have no idea who could have been so cruel to do this. Peach was one of the good guys."

With that, Bridge wiped his eye. The room was now empty, as the small group of well-wishers were on their way back to their cars and lives.

"Madame, do you think that we could talk for a minute?"

Young Shark sensed something in the air that hung like thick humidity.

"Cousin Bridge. I'll wait outside with our group", said the future captain and smuggler.

To which Bridge replied, "Nah, kid. Stay with me while I console Madame Peach. To see such a handsome young man might bring her some cheer."

Madame nodded and warily smiled.

Bridge began, "Your husband and I were partners for years. He was a great man, and I can't understand how such a tragedy would befall him."

"Thank you, Captain Bridge. He always spoke highly of you and the guys."

Bridge nodded in appreciation and continued, "As you know, he was a successful, self-made entrepreneur. And for that, of course, he deserves respect. Not just in life, but now at the time of his unfortunate passing.

"I know this probably isn't the time or place, but I did want to reach out and say that as we are both aware, your husband and I shared certain business interests. I was hoping to discuss these matters as we now find ourselves as partners, and hopefully can continue to expand upon your husband's vision."

The room was eerily quiet as there were only four of them, if Peach's corpse counted.

Madame suddenly appeared nervous, yet maintained an air of confidence. It was as if her keen instincts knew that there was no way that Bridge was walking out of the funeral home without discussing the future.

She never loved Peach, but she tolerated his rogue behavior due to a genuine love of a lifestyle that included Maseratis and pony-aged lovers. The marriage and subsequent business partnership were just that.

An exercise in capitalism.

"Bridge, I know that you have certain expectations due to

my husband's passing, and what that might mean to his prior business arrangements.

"But I must say, as his widow and only heir, I wish that I could say that I could continue working with you, but your financial demands of Peach these past few years were rather lofty in the eyes of many around me."

Shark was not scared. Rather, he found himself in that early teen state of first arousal.

"Bridge, I was already approached by a group from Miami who are willing to do the distribution deal with me, and I still get to keep all of my assets and current arrangements.

"Your deal, I'm quite certain based on the recent dealings with my late beloved, would leave me, well, rather thin.

"I'm sorry Bridge. I wish that we could work together, but I'm really left with no option. Peach would agree that it's just good business."

Bridge was quiet, but his stare grew more intense as he cleared his throat.

Madame slowly shook her head, "He was such a generous and forward-thinking soul. Why, to share his success with the blacks and even Orientals like this boy you brought? Well, that takes a man of true vision."

Young Shark was now beginning to shake.

"I now need to focus on business. Thank you for coming to say good-bye to Peach. And Bridge, for one moment, please do not believe that I'm unaware of your role in his untimely demise."

Cousin Bridge remained solemn, as one should in the confines of a funeral home. He hosted thoughts. He contemplated.

"You're right, Madame. Shame on me for broaching the subject at this time. We're in a tough business, and why make it more difficult for anyone?

"I wish you well on your new opportunity. I'm sure that

you'll do quite well, as we all know that you were backbone of Peach's success."

Madame exhaled, and seemed to relax.

"You mentioned my saying goodbye to him, Madame. May I for one last time?"

"Of course, Captain." Madame said with a sigh of relief at being able to avoid a difficult situation. While more at ease, she still could not wait for Bridge to vacate her presence.

Bridge summoned his nephew, "Kid, be a man and come over to pray and offer proper respects to my old friend. Kneel with me and say a Hail Mary."

Shark did as he was instructed and knelt beside his cousin. They gazed over the remains of a man who Bridge seemingly respected.

Shark began in a low voice, "Hail Mary, full of grace. The Lord is with Thee. Blessed, art thou…"

As Shark prayed, Bridge suddenly reached under Peach's casket pillow and pulled out the Baretta M9 that he earlier had planted by the funeral director with clear instruction and a bag of cash. Bridge hoped that things could have been resolved amicably and that the weapon would have been buried forever along with Peach. Unfortunately for Madame, she threw the dice and rolled a seven.

Bridge spun around to face the widow.

"Sister, you were always the brains. But your husband will forever be the heart."

"Wait!" screamed Madame, "Wait! You will wait. No!"

"Sorry, bitch. Time and tide…"

And with that, Bridge squeezed the trigger. One half of Madam's head remained perfectly still, while the other smashed a fake Monet off the wall.

Chapter 9

OceanView Hotel

Shark returned from his Cousin Bridge daydream.

Subtle yet direct, Shark and Peeler were approached by a distinguished looking gentleman in a finely tailored Armani suit. A suit not conducive to the sweltering weather conditions, yet perfect for the hotel's turbo-charged A/C.

"Gentlemen, my name is Carlos. Thank you so much for joining us in beautiful Bal Harbour. I trust that your passage was one of fair travel, and we certainly appreciate your efforts. Mr. Conzalez cares to conduct your meeting upstairs in his suite where you will be assured comfort and the utmost privacy."

Shark responded quickly, "Hey, Chuck. The meeting happens here, or my colleague and I are throwing our lines in five minutes."

Carlos took a deep breath. "As you wish Captain, please give me a few minutes to notify Mr. Conzalez that you care to take dinner in the main dining room."

Shark thought for a second, then simply out of curiosity changed his mind, "Ah, fuck it Chuck. I want to see his fancy digs in this joint. Where's the elevator?"

Chapter 10

Lu-Lu on her cell phone

"Hey Shred, how ya been, baby?" asked a half-stoned Lu-Lu after spending the night with Gerbil Turner.

"Wow, sweets. It's great to hear from you. How's everything going? Still keeping the ice cold and the cans firm?"

"Yeah, Shred. Trying to hold it together and if I must say, I think I'm doing a pretty damn good job."

With pleasantries aside, Lu-Lu continued, "Shred, remember you told me if during my travels, should I ever come across what could be viewed as a decent score, you'd cut me in on the deal?"

Shred responded, "I'll only remember if the deal is any good. If it's shit, then I might have a sudden case of dementia and start gnawing on my remote. Why, whaddaya think you got?"

"Well, I was with this guy. Actually, I've been with him quite a bit."

Shred interjected, "Business or pleasure, Lu?"

"Oh, definitely business. He's bizarre, but he treats me fine and all. He always settles up his tab properly, but he's really out there and I'm not exactly fresh off the turnip truck if you follow me?"

"Proceed," responded a curious Shred.

"Anyway, he likes to talk big, so I'm not exactly sure how much credence there is to this. Apparently there's some kind of on-going scheme based out of Port Side Vow that he's knee deep in, and he was bragging about the money they were pulling in."

"What type of score, Lu? Smack?" asked a wary Shred.

"No, it sounds like some kind of counterfeiting operation. I dunno, a money thing. I just wanted to call you 'cause you said that if I ever get a whiff of a score, that I should reach out. And more importantly, that I'd get paid if it's real. I wouldn't mind a Porsche like yours someday."

Shred responded, "Hmm. This one sounds unique. And as you know, nobody has a right to make money in our backyard without my group getting its fair share. It's only proper etiquette. Ya know, it's just the American way. I need more information though, toots."

Shred loved the smell of opportunity, and had ever since he decided that by divine right he would involve himself in all waterfront illegal activity. At a paltry height of five foot five inches, Shred did not exactly cast a menacing presence, however those that knew him best were aware that the most frightening and dangerous part of him resided above the eyeballs. While many believed that his nickname stemmed from his big-wave surfing acumen, it was actually due to his ability to make hard-core decisions and execute jobs that often involved violence, be it necessary or symbolic.

Some believed that this unpredictable demeanor was due to a lifelong Napoleon complex, which was certainly a contributor, but his extreme nature was more a reflection of his upbringing.

He was orphaned as a baby and any records of his actual parents went missing, either by accident or otherwise. After shuffling from orphanages to foster homes and back, he eventually caught the attention of one of his counselors who saw potential in the fiery, intelligent youth.

The counselor assisted Shred in finding a permanent home with a foster family who had an excellent track record with the State of Georgia. Jog and Patty Wilson took in the twelve-year old Shred and treated him as one of their own.

Shred would escort Jog Wilson each morning during school break down to the docks in order to pick up fresh Summer Flounder and Black Sea Bass. The supply would be sold immediately that day at Wilson's Fish Market in the small coastal town of Shellman Bluff. Jog always took immense pride in the quality of his wares as his father and grandfather did for decades. Life was sedate and simple, and Shred enjoyed the closest existence to what resembled a normal childhood. It was a bucolic backdrop that he had never experienced before, and never would again.

One morning, earlier than usual Jog called for Shred to get ready and to meet him in the truck. A boat had just arrived at the dock with an especially large haul of famous Georgia Weakfish. As usual, Jog wanted first dibs on the prime cuts and brought along a burlap bag full of cash in order to transact business quickly and quietly. He was forever fearful of alerting the attention of any of the state wildlife regulators or tax jackals who might also be eyeing the prized catch.

It was no secret that most business transactions within their dying industry were based on hard cash and handshakes. When Shred was a kid he seldom heard of any trouble or crime down in that area. It was an age old micro-economy that fed and protected its own system's ability to endure while shrugging off modern advances in commerce.

However, like most symbiotic environments, over time word gets out and someone crashes the party.

The two headed to the docks in Jog's old Ford pick-up that by now was held together by duck tape and chicken wire. They took a remote back road in order to avail themselves to a shortcut, but also to avoid the attention of the County Sheriff's officers who might be curious to see if the old junker could actually pass state inspection.

As a whistling Jog drove east at around fifty miles an hour, suddenly an oversized white Chevy van pulled out from the woods and blocked the road. Jog had to slam on the brakes, only to notice a similar vehicle pull out to block a rear getaway.

"Pah, what's goin' on here?" asked a jumpy Shred who by nature was easily spooked.

Trying to keep the air calm, Jog replied, "Just sit still, son. They prob'ly just needin' some directions."

Jog slowly opened the truck door after instructing Shred to sit tight. The windows were open so Shred could hear every word of the exchange.

"Well, well, Mr. Wilson. Looks here like you be headin' east? Any reason why? And hell, in such a rush with this old heap on wheels. Why, I'd be afraid these here bumps and stumps in the road might rattle off every nut and bolt on this ol' scrapper."

Jog remained quiet, as he did not want to upset Shred.

"Jog, we both know that you got a bit of cash in that there bag in the back, and I do notice that you have a little boy in the front. Now, it would seem to me that a reasonable man like yourself would just assume end this day as gentle as it began?"

Jog was shocked that the grease-smeared guy knew his name. While he did not recognize his assumed bandit, or his cronies who were slowly surrounding the vehicle, he had heard rumors about some ruffian Florida boys who'd been entering the state and who were up to no good due to the layoffs on the farms.

Jog calmly replied, "Sir, I dunno who you are or where you are from, but your van is in my way, and I'm not looking for any trouble. Why don't we all just get back in our vehicles and go 'bouts our business?"

"Well Mr. Wilson, now we are all in agreement and making sense like gentlemen. Ain't that right boys?" The bandit's men nodded and grunted in affirmation.

"Ya' see Jog, that's exactly what we all want to do and will. However, before we can initiate such a courtesy as to allow you to pass, we must be compensated for our troubles. In my humble opinion, a fair compromise would be if you give us that old bag in the rear. We'll then get back in our vans and go 'bouts our way, while wishing you and your son a pleasant rest of the day."

Despite Shred's young age, he knew exactly what was happening. They were being robbed of their much-needed money to procure the day's fresh catch. While these bandits did appear potentially dangerous in appearance and demeanor, Shred noticed that no weapons had been drawn. Perhaps, their sheer numbers gave them the confidence and comfort that they would not need to go to such extends to pull off this simple job.

Shred hoped that might prove to be a mistake.

Shred also noticed that on the floor of the truck was Jog's old Smith & Wesson Magnum which he always kept loaded and ready just in case he ran into a dangerous or wounded animal. While the bandit's attention was fully focused on Jog, Shred quietly picked up the weapon and held it against his right thigh. While he was in no way a sharp-shooter, he had done enough practice with Jog that he was confident of being able to extricate them from this situation.

The bandit continued to reason with Jog, who was steadfast that the cash-filled sack was to remain in tact and aboard the truck. It was only then that the robber brandished a large, shiny machete that looked like it had been recently sharpened and polished.

Shred angled his body against the passenger door without being noticed.

The bandit continued, "Now, Mr. Wilson…"

Shred leaned out of the passenger window and,

BLAST!!

The Magnum's .357 slug exploded the grill of the blocking van, surely causing serious engine damage.

The bandit crew was completely taken by surprise, with some running to the rear van to fetch their own weapons, however Shred was not going to allow for that much time.

Shred screamed, "Git in the truck, Pah! Let's go! Now!"

And with that Shred twisted further out of the passenger window and leaned his lanky torso over the top of the truck. He took aim and unloaded the next round in the leader's direction.

BLAM!!

As the slug ripped into the bandit's shoulder, his screams shattered the peace of hundreds of birds who immediately fled from the trees in panic.

The bandit lay on the ground in excruciating pain. Jog quickly looked him over and was surprised that while Shred's shot definitely ruined the guy's pitching career, his wound was not lethal.

Jog could immediately tell that they were not dealing with professionals. The bandit's "loyal" crew screamed off in the rear van casting dirt and rocks across a fifty yard radius.

"Let's get outta here, boy!" Jog yelled as loud as he ever had at his adopted son. With the bandit still lying on the road in agony, Jog got in and punched the gas pedal. He and Shred pushed that old truck as fast as she would go in a direct easterly trajectory.

"You shouldn't have done that, boy!" Jog was still yelling and panicked.

"What's gonna happen to him, Pah?"

"Oh hell, boy. We'll tell one of the ladies at the bait shop that we heard there was an accident on this road. The authorities will be out here soon, and I'd just assume that we not be around to see it!"

Shred was proud that he had saved Jog, but instinctively his racing mind told him that long-term he would become a danger and a liability a man who did not deserve the heat. That thought occurred to Shred the second that he fired the weapon, for it frightened yet excited him at how natural it felt. He enjoyed it way too much.

Years later, from the lessons learned as a kid in a survivor's environment, Shred bullied and depended on information from prostitutes like Lu-Lu, while also from a few low-level drug peddlers who bottom fed for information within shoreline communities. The big guys who controlled the larger rackets and illegal enterprises in Savannah viewed Shred as more of a nuisance and thorn in their sides. He was never taken seriously as a player and was still considered to be a swamp rat. However, over the years he managed to eke out a living while maintaining a low profile, despite some of his violent tendencies.

Other players in the criminal realm could look down on Shred all they wanted, but nobody could take away the fact that the guy was a risk-taker and a consummate survivor of the odds. Kind of like a cockroach.

Chapter 11
OceanView Hotel, Bal Harbour

Carlos pressed "P" on the elevator keypad. As he stepped back, Shark and Peeler warily watched his every move. It was one thing to meet with known gangsters in a public venue, but now they were heading backstage.

Shark was intrigued by the prospect of meeting Don Juan Conzalez. His reputation called for operations that involved an abnormally high level of risk, but with the potential of a lucrative payday. However, he knew to proceed with caution, a key reason why the seasoned captain was still roaming life's quarterdeck, and not serving as bait in a crab trap.

As the elevator door opened into Conzalez's penthouse foyer, Peeler could not help but feel the envy at how the other half lived. He regretted not studying harder in school, though he knew that the type of education received by a man like Juan Conzalez was impossible to receive within the confines of academia.

They were greeted at the door by two armed guardaespaldas, and were led through the middle of the palatial penthouse to the entrance of the balcony where Juan, dressed in a white linen suit, waited with a table full of mojitos, iced tea and fresh fruit.

The vast room leading to the balcony, while the size of an airport gateway, was much differently appointed. Though the space was splashed in the purest of whites, it was in no way reminiscent of an institution. Large paintings adorned the immaculate walls, and radiated deep purples, stark jade greens and small blasts of sunrise orange. The decor complemented the gold-framed mirrors, while the lavender and peach antique vases served as tasteful accents.

"Gentlemen, it is with my sincere appreciation that you accepted my invitation on such short notice. Please sit and help yourself to a cold refreshment. If there is anything else that you need, do not hesitate to ask Carlos and he will be more than happy to accommodate you."

Shark poured himself an iced tea and tossed in a lemon wedge, while Peeler helped himself to a two-dram glassful of a Bacardi Millennium mojito with freshly cut lime and mint leaves.

The deckhand savored the first sip of the rare rum, for he knew that one bottle cost more than he usually made in a month.

Shark sat in his chair while sliding it into the shade.

"Don Conzalez, it is with respect and gratitude that I accepted your invitation, but I must admit that I am a little confused. I certainly know of your vast business empire, and apparently you've learned a bit about mine. I can't imagine a man in your position who is so revered in our unruly arena, would gain much from a minor league player like myself and my rum-enthused colleague."

Shark looked over at his partner who was unabashedly star-ing at the runway-worthy Latina named Jillian, who had come in to freshen up the mojito jug. Clearly Peeler was going to be as much help in this meeting as a knife at a carbine fight.

Conzalez smiled and responded, "Captain Bertolami, I will explain. While I do know of your various business lines, and yes, I must admit that even though you are known to be industrious and successful in your ventures, it's true that I tend to deal with larger contractors on my projects. But this one is unique and requires someone, let's just say, who is a bit off the radars of both the good and the bad guys, as well as anyone else in between."

Shark cleared his throat, "So, you're considering hiring me because you consider my operation minor league? Not sure that my aging pride likes the sound of that one."

"Captain, I mean you no offense. It is merely more strategic and practical to engage someone who might not attract the type of attention that I want to avoid while we pull off one of the more unique opportunities that I have encountered in quite a while. It's just good business, Senor Tiburon. You will understand in a moment why this project is so near to my heart.

"And you, as well as your partner here with the swollen eyes on my niece, stand to profit handsomely."

"I'm listening," responded a stoic-faced Shark.

"Captain, I will tell you the story, and then only you can decide if it's a job which interests you. You see, yes, I do enjoy a prosperous import business, but I do face obstacles like any major player in any other industry. And I'm not referring to just the Coast Guard and Homeland Security, who as we know are basically one in the same these days. They are easy to elude and actually easier to bribe in certain cases. I'm referring to, and am more concerned with, my competitors. Contrary to certain beliefs, I'm not the only importer in South Florida, and have not been for several years. And trust me in that when an adversary in my profession decides to scuttle one of my operations, they do not recite the Miranda Rights. They stab you in the left eye, and then let the right side watch as you are fed through a bait grinder."

Shark was quiet for a moment before responding, "Don Conzalez, I understand that you're not about to ask us to take your nephews Mahi fishing. I'm listening."

"Captain, one of the competitors in my business is a most worthy adversary. He recently procured a shipment of highly valuable cargo in Cartagena. The exact contents of the run, I am not certain, but I know it contained a large city's annual supply of opiates, cocaine and heroin. None of the pesky marijuana bales that take up too much transport space. Plus, la mierda is getting legalized anyway in the States, thus destroying a somewhat valuable product line. It's not what it used to be, but I digress, and am not one to lament over the so-called good old days."

Shark shifted in his chair as to listen more intently.

"The ship in question left Columbia with the goal of traveling west of Cuba, then making a wide arc around South Florida to avoid the attention of authorities. They were to next rendezvous with a smaller vessel that would carry the cargo to Nassau for a brief layover until the heat died down. The eventual goal was a straight and unimpeded bolt to Miami."

Shark rubbed his chin, "You seem to know a lot about the intricacies of your competitor's operations."

"I do my homework, Captain. The key is that my competitor has his own adversaries, some even within his own organization. Loyalty can be rare these days. At any rate, someone within his crew ratted out the run to a third party. Not a wise decision on his part. Once my competitor learned of the duplicity, the first mate who committed the betrayal was laid out on the deck in front of his peers.

"Do you know anything about marine electricity, Captain Shark?"

"Yeah, sorta. Juan, where's this going?"

"You Americans and your lack of patience. Anyway, the scoundrel who foolishly shared the details of the project had his scrotum wired to all four of the vessel's marine batteries. Supposedly, when the switch was thrown it was not pretty, however he did glow and would have been handy at Christmas. He actually did not shake that violently despite the voltage. Perhaps, it was the counter-action of the rubber fishing boots?

"Yet, I digress once again... a sign of my advancing years.

"The traitor shared the travel plans with another of our other competitors. Thus, the ship was pirated and all the contraband disappeared like someone tossing ashes into the wind.

"So, Captain Bertolami… By the way, with all due respect, how does a Chinaman get a Guinea name? I find it most curious."

Shark paused and cleared his throat, pulling out every stop in order to maintain decorum.

"My mother was from the Mekong Delta. My old man, from Polermo. That okay with you, Senor?"

Conzalez's hand gently waved to calm the air. "I see, I see. Please take no offense. An interesting union, nonetheless.

"Anyway, the purpose of my story is that I'm sharing this information in anticipation of your finding the missing haul for me which, in turn, will potentially provide us both a substantial bounty."

"How much you talking, Conzalez, and why me?"

"Because Captain, I am told that you are the best at what you do, and that you keep your mouth shut. Of course if you don't, you will be the prison cell-mate of a starved bull shark within minutes of any transgression."

"Okay, Juan. What are you offering besides the price of getting an F in Conduct?"

"All right, all right, Captain. My offer is simple. Money, and lots of it."

Shark nodded, "Alright. Now you're making sense. So, how does this roll?"

"My competitor's vessel got pirated on the way from Cartagena in waters off the Florida coast.

"There was a violent exchange that left both crews dead and millions of dollars of product falling into the bottom of the ocean in water-tight containers.

"Anyway, amidst all of the unnecessary violence that afternoon, I now know of a certain dive site where the cargo was lost."

Shark could not stop laughing.

"Are you out of your mind, Juan? With your resources, just send a boat out and grab the shit. I smell a classic fish story. By the way, how the hell did you find out where the shit is if everyone was left for dead on sinking ships?

"No offense, but I mean, just go out and grab it yourself. 'Da fuck am I missing here?"

The seasoned contraband captain was quickly beginning to lose his banana-wind temper, even in the presence of a man like Juan Conzalez.

"With all due respect Captain, I assume that we will both ignore your outburst. Regarding my knowledge of the location, let's just say that perhaps there may have been one survivor who eventually died, but happened to be one of my spies and radioed in to us the location. He did this in exchange for the promise of a handsome payment to his wife and children after his soon-to-be demise. As a man of honor, I will see to that, but overall it is not your concern how I gained such information."

Shark nodded to express his understanding.

"Regarding my just grabbing it, you see it's not that simple. I cannot attract the slightest bit of attention, and at the moment all eyes are on my operation from Bogota to Boston. All components of my activities are under strict instructions: men, boats, trucks, planes and mistresses. I cannot have anyone in my organization near that dive site. I only trust you and your ability to make this happen, and to happen most surreptitiously."

Shark nodded his head slowly as Conzalez continued, "We could be great partners. Your take would be about two million. That's about ten percent. The rest is mine for serving as general contractor and information broker."

Peeler remained uncharacteristically quiet while enjoying his rum. He knew that Shark was in negotiation mode and to break his concentration would mean a tongue-lashing that would last the duration of the cruise home.

"Don Conzalez," began Shark, "What you're offering at first glance appears most generous. Let me ask you, despite my reputation and your confidence in my abilities, what if by chance I cannot deliver your contraband? What happens if Peel and I are left floating out there for three days with our pricks in our hands?

"Maybe it's a silly question, but do I still get my two million?"

The Don responded, "Captain, while you most likely know the answer to that, I am happy to clarify. If you fail in this assignment, and it's not of your own doing, I will pay you triple your highest charter rate for however many hours you are out on the water. That seems a generous reward for lack of success."

Shark quickly responded, "Juan, how do you know how long we will have been out there, and how hard we've tried? I might just soak you for a three day charter and tie the boat up in South Beach. I'll let ol' Peeler here enjoy a three-day rum bender, while I will perhaps enjoy the fine company of one of the local ladies. On your dime."

Conzalez leaned back and replied, "If you fail and the mission is compromised by your own purposeful actions, or perhaps you are to disappear in the Bermuda Triangle by choice, then the consequences will of course be of a violent nature for you and your first mate. Please trust that the level of severity will make Satan himself blush."

Conzalez sipped on his ice tea to calm the air.

"But, Captain. From what I am told, you are a serious man. The scenario that you describe would be short-sighted, and not to mention unnecessarily dangerous. You are well aware that I have friends with eyes and ears all over Florida and the Islands. More importantly, you want the two million, and with no disrespect, the word on the street is that you could use it."

Shark tilted his head as Conzalez continued, "I should also mention that you'll be required as per our contract, to bring along a second mate who will answer to only you for the duration of the voyage. There will be no need for her to check in with my organization every day. From what I understand, Captain, is that you play hard-ball, but are not a murderer unless the situation calls for such severe measures. That will not be the case with the woman who I'm assigning to be under your temporary, but full command."

Shark shot back, "Hold on, Juan. A woman? I don't need any more ballast, nor some nautical babysitter. Plus, a woman aboard a voyage is bad luck unless she's made of wood and nailed to the bow."

"Oh, but I insist Captain. I like to have my projects monitored at all times. In this case, I will send someone who might attract certain attention, but not the kind of attention that would raise awareness as to the nature of your endeavors. As a matter of fact, she is with us here today. I trust that you noticed my niece, Jillian, assisting with the refreshments. She will provide the surveillance that I demand, not request, and will not look like a hired goon to anyone who's curious as to your activities."

Shark merely nodded. He knew that this component to the assignment would not be negotiable, and he was catching himself in an amateur moment of already envisioning the two million.

Conzalez continued, "Please understand that she's no babe in the woods. She can handle an AK-47 and stiletto as well as any MI6 spook. She'll remain onboard during the operation and will report directly to you at all times.

"Please know Captain, with all due respect, that while I have no concerns about your intentions as I know you are a formidable businessman. But should your first-mate, Mr. Peeler so much as touch a stray hair on Jillian's shoulder in even the most innocent of approaches, I will remove each of his fingers over a few days' course. He will suffer greatly, but that time will allow him to ponder the consequences of his lack of discretion and professionalism."

Shark shifted in his chair, yet remained quiet.

The description of such a punishment made Peeler reach to stiffen his drink.

Shark was quiet and deep in thought. This was no simple offer, but an enticement with a bit of a command performance element, blended like a sordid daiquiri of opportunities.

"Don Conzalez, your offer is intriguing and appreciated. If you could indulge me, would you grant the flexibility of twenty-four hours in order to contemplate logistics and feasibility, and then at which time I'll give you a formal response. I'm not playing games, as you know that's not my style. I just want to be certain that I can deliver. I am taking this offer seriously and need to consider the many angles. This isn't exactly a Sunday whale-watch charter."

Juan leaned back in his chair, "Captain Shark, I expected you to be a serious man, and you have proven so by your request for time to consider. I would appreciate a response by this time tomorrow. When you contact me, please demand that you speak to me personally as per my request. Do not mention anything to anyone in my organization."

Sharks eyebrows perked up a bit.

"Juan, you suspect a breach of confidentiality on this well-run, tightest of ships?"

"Captain, let's just say that I am a careful man. Anyone other than a careful man would not have survived and prospered for so long in this business. During my life I have served merely one night in jail as a foolish young man who acted as such one evening drowned in Havana spiced rum and spicier perfume."

Shark slightly chuckled.

"I shall await your call, Captain Shark. It has been a pleasure making your acquaintance and sharing your company."

Shark replied, "Don Conzalez, you've been a gracious host, and your generosity spills over into your offer. I won't make you wait another minute past this time tomorrow. If you don't mind, Peeler and I would like to try and make it back before dark. If your gentleman could see us out?"

And with that, Shark and Peeler headed back to the Booty Call, the captain with a heavy, thought-laden head, and the first mate enjoying a warm afternoon rum buzz.

As they walked down the dock, Peeler broke the silence.

"Hey, Skip. How do ya think that hot little niece would look like under me rollin' around in the ol' bunkroom?" asked the exited mate.

"I dunno, Peel." responded Shark, "Probably like Phyllis Diller on a bobsled."

Chapter 12

Port Side Vow Marina, Jekyll Island

As Justin battled with a fitful sleep, he jarred from side to side while falling in and out of a dream…

The smell from the fire assaulted his nose and burned his tearing eyes. While the thickness of the smoke had diminished, it still shrouded the field before him and altered the blackness of the ground from a pure charcoal hue to a rainbow of grays and dirty whites.

Jus treaded lightly with each step so as to not trip over the pieces of smoldering wood left behind from what once appeared to have been a large house. With each crunch under his steps, he inhaled proof of the horrifying possibility that this was indeed his work. His destruction. His creation.

"Damn!" Jus said quickly as he lost his footing on an object that at first glance, looked like a piece of a mannequin or child's doll. He bent down to pick up the warm artifact, when he suddenly realized that it was a small leg. Fortunately for Jus, it was not a real appendage, but it was a cast that may have served as a souvenir after having been removed from a once broken leg injury. As Jus rubbed the thick soot off of the small, thin, fiberglass object, it revealed its true bright pink color. Scribbled on it

with the handwriting of little fingers were the simple names that children use. "Grandma", "Papa" and "Mommy". Also, written in a darker marker color was the word "Daddy", which looked like someone had attempted scratch it out before the fire.

For some reason, Jus felt compelled to place the cast in a small knapsack that he was carrying, and continued on crunching through the rubble. He carefully walked another fifty yards or so and noticed a plate in the middle of crumbled embers that for some reason had less of the soot and burn damage that seemed to engulf everything around him.

It was a blueish/gray plate with bright colored lettering that had three words spelled out vertically, but because the object was marred, very little of the lettering remained legible. It reminded Jus of a child's art class project, and if he really squinted, he could make out the three words:

"World's

Best

Daddy."

Due to the fire damage, the letters that appeared most legible were:

"Wor***

**st

Da**y"

Justin merely stared, but felt compelled to place the trinket in his bag.

He looked around and nothing else seemed to have survived the blaze. He wondered who had set the fire and why? More baffling, was how he ended up here surveying the damage?

Then, a girl's soft whisper breezed by and felt gentle on his face. At first, he could not make out the words, but the air was comforting and warm, and carried a fragrance that was more pleasant than the stench of scorched wood and earth.

With each caressing breeze, the whisper proved more audible.

"Ar... s... "

"on…"
The voice grew louder.
"Ars…"
"Arson…"
The voice became disturbingly more pronounced.
"Arson… Justin… Arson… Daddy? Arson… Why, Daddy? Why, arson?"
"Why, burn?… Burn hurts so much, Daddy… Why, burn? Why, arson?"
"Do you burn too, Daddy? Do you hurt like us?" "Do you burn like us?"
"HUH! WHAT!"

Justin violently stirred and jerked up in bed. Breathing heavy, he looked around in order to gather his bearings. He quickly realized that another uninvited nightmare had visited and that it was dark and quiet as he lay next to Marlene. He carefully pushed the sheets away and left the bed while making every effort not to disturb his lover. He quietly exited the stateroom for much needed topside open air.

About an hour later, Marl awoke.

She rolled over and suddenly realized that she had overslept, but figured on that being acceptable in light of the events of the past few days.

Marlene had new items added to her thought menu. A risky business venture that her partner and lover seemed to embrace more and more by the hour, plus her pitch to Justin for them to look after Michonne for the near future.

It was a lot to process. Especially, for a mind that had endured so much in the past year, not the least of which was the fact that the man who professed his love for her, pulled a trigger that almost snatched her life.

These were the ghosts who greeted Marl as her day began.

She got up and proceeded to Free Lance's galley where she began brewing a fresh pot of Hazelnut grinds. At this point in her life, she gained solace from simple things. She loved her flavored coffee as much as she loved flipping over her pillow during a hot summer night to find that welcomed coolness.

With java brewed, and cream and sugar added, she headed topside in order to find Justin quietly sitting at the end of the dock and looking out over the harbor whose apathy taunted his already jilted thoughts.

Marl sat next to him and greeted his heavy head with a soft kiss on the side of his neck.

"Nice sun," remarked Marl, "Is that why you're staring right into it?"

Justin switched his sitting position on the dock in order to better receive Marl's reassuring touch.

"I dunno, Marl. Just thinking. Just thinking about our future and where we're going. Whadda we doing? Who we wanna be?"

Marlene listened and stroked his wavy hair.

"Marl, it's this opportunity with Shark. I think it could be a solid score, but I realize that you have reservations and I trust your instincts."

Marl moved her hand to cover his, "Jus, I've been thinking. You're likely right that running plates is gonna grow stale and will end up a defunct business.

"Here's my thought. I suggest we tell Shark that we'll try it once. And agree to only once. We snag Gerbil, and see how it goes. He's so friggin' nuts that if we throw enough money at him, hopefully any of the human risk factors will be diminished. Our main concern will be the Coast Guard, but there are others. What if one of these people is carrying around friggin Ebola or some shit? And of course, a bigger more obvious concern is a damned mutiny."

Justin exhaled a slow, long strand of air.

Marlene continued, "But I guess if we make enough room so that we can transport twenty of these poor souls, we gross eighty grand."

As the couple debated the human contraband operation, the slow clip-clop of feet wrapped in oversized sandals was so loud that it scared off the ducks lumbering on the dock.

"Michonne, good morning." Marlene immediately sported a happy face, "How'd you sleep, honey?"

Michonne was still scratching her eyes, "I'm okay. It was so comfortable on your boat. The little waves rocked me right to sleep." She then paused and looked at Marl. "I'm kinda hungry."

Marl stood up and in an unusual motherly role and replied, "No problem, honey. Stay with Justin and I'll be right back."

Michonne took Marl's place on the dock next to Boston's most wanted assassin-at-large, and slowly gazed at him.

"I know you don't like me Mr. Justin. I don't blame you, cause nobody likes me. But I like you and Miss Marlene."

Justin gazed at the once mud-ridden urchin turned yacht stowaway and responded, "Please, don't say that. I like you, Michonne. I like you very much. You're a survivor, and survivors are the ones who will make it in this world. Everything will be fine if you stick tight to Marlene. I have. Indeed, I have."

Justin's mind began to wander but the little girl brought him back.

"Mr. Justin. I know that you and Marlene are busy with something. I can tell, and I can help. I want to help 'cause you've been so nice to me and let me stay somewhere where nobody yells at me."

He couldn't argue with such logic. Justin marveled how even though her physical image reflected a girl a few years older, she still had a little girl's sensibility. Despite appearing to have accumulated a long resume within a short life, she still maintained a streak of innocence.

"Michonne, honey. Marl and I have some adult things to work out, but in the meantime just focus on being a little girl."

Justin knew that if the world had not stolen that sentiment from her already, it inevitably would.

Chapter 13

Brush/Shrub area across from PSV Marina

"So Lu-Lu, tell me again. This is where a counterfeiting operation is being stationed? Looks to me like a bunch of wharf rats whose tuna balls are the only things onboard larger than their livers," quipped Shred.

The pair looked on from across the marina in a make-shift encampment that they established on the banks of a deep salt pond.

Other than the fact that the mosquitoes bit like hacksaws, it was a pleasant enough spot from which to observe Marlene and Justin. And now, the little girl.

"Hey, toots," said Shred as he stared into the binoculars. "You didn't tell me they had a daughter. Who the hell is that? Take a look."

Shred handed Lu-Lu the binocs into which she peered and quickly gave them back.

"Fuck if I know, Shred. Gerbil never mentioned a kid."

Shred shrugged his shoulders. Kid or no kid, he was not going to let anything get in the way of tapping into profits that were being enjoyed in his neighborhood. A brush up on the local rules was duly needed.

Normally, Shred turned a blind eye to the drunken two-bit dime bag peddlers at Port Side Vow, but counterfeiting was something unique to Shred, and it smelled of an opportunity sweeter than the best ganja that they could import from Mo' Bay.

Shred continued, "So my dear, you gathered your intel from that wet brain of Gerbil's, but contend that it's a score. And you guarantee that you told me everything. Everything, Lu?"

"Yeah, Shred. Once I smelled somethin' in it for me, I called you right away. I want a piece of the action, and while Gerbil is crazy and all, he always seems to have money to pay for pulling my panties."

That caused Shred to suddenly chuckle, "Ha! Bogus money for a bogus mistress. Fuckin' Aye."

Shred refocused, "Okay, Lu. But again, you're sure that everything you know is now in my ears and that you firmly believe this is worth the time and mosquito welts?"

"Yeah, Shred. I would not withhold anything from you. Anything."

And with that Lu-Lu placed a hand on Shred's thigh and began to rub him above his shorts.

Shred took a deep breath and lay down in the deep grass that ran the parameter of the salt pond. He moaned gently as Lu-Lu was quite industrious in her willingness to please.

Shred continued as he fumbled for his duffel bag, "Lu, my dear. I need to fetch a toy from my bag. It's something you'll enjoy."

Lu could already feel the stiffness of the sex toys that Shred would often bestow upon her. Frankly, she preferred them to Shred's usual lackluster performance in the bedroom. His mind was often a million miles away even as she begged in three languages for his climax.

Shred was thoroughly convinced that he had extracted all of the information that Lu-Lu could provide, and within a Clark

Kent phone booth moment of transformation, Lu morphed from being a valued asset into a dangerously knowledgeable liability.

He dipped into the bag as Lu-Lu slowly kissed his stomach and then headed south. She was convinced that this time would be different.

She was correct.

Shred extracted an six-inch buck knife from his duffel and quietly held it behind his head as Lu-Lu proceeded to please him with the utmost fervor.

He gently caressed her soft hair as he looked up and saw a bald eagle trading trees. Slowly, he held Lu's head a bit more firmly, and she figured that he was about to explode.

Suddenly in a quick motion, Shred pulled Lu up by her hair and slid the knife across her jugular. As her blood burst a geyser shot across Shred's chest, no sound could be heard. No crying. No yelling. Just the silent scream of death. As he pulled her head up by the hair, he gazed into empty eyes. Eyes that only moments ago radiated dreams.

He got up, fixed his shorts and wiped the weapon clean. As he further opened the duffel, he tried to justify his actions in that he just saved Lu-Lu from a continued life of frustration and disappointment.

She had served her purpose.

"Shit! Where's the damn chain?" Shred hissed at the eagle as he sifted through the bag.

As he finally extricated the metal links, he coiled them around Lu's neck like an Amazon boa.

He stared at her.

Such a beautiful creation. At one time, so innocent. Yet, so ambitious which was the downfall of everyone, thought Shred. Lu had made an informant's greatest mistake - letting the client think that you have nothing left to share.

With a gentle shove, he watched as his young informant sank peacefully into the dark depths of the salt pond, only to never serve as an informant again. Shred subtly smiled as he realized an uplifting side to his deed, as Lu would now serve as much needed nourishment for days to come for the creatures of this forsaken ecosystem.

"The circle of life…" hummed Shred.

As he took a deep breath, his mind floated back to his days as a boy after he ran away from Jog Wilson. Jog was the closest person that Shred ever had to a father, and that is why he knew that he needed to leave in order to protect him. Shred ended up in the tough Adamsville section of Atlanta. He lived in a one room tenement with a woman who he met in a park who seemed to take pity on the lonesome Shred. She slept all day while each evening she used the one lone bedroom as her place of entrepreneurial commerce. She was (or had at least convinced the neighbors of the fact) the illegitimate daughter of Marie Therese Alourdes Macena Champagne Lovinski, commonly known as American's most famous Voodoo high priestess, Mama Lola.

She had a booming business and used her spurious mother's moniker for marketing purposes. She often spent her nights locked away in the bedroom chanting and making a racket. She would clank together precious gems (rocks from the sand lot across the street), burn and boil the bones of rare breeds of animals smuggled in from Haiti, that in actuality were chicken scraps that Shred collected from the alley behind Wing World Take-Out. Neighbors would stop by with cash and jewelry and beg Mama to cast spells on their enemies near and abroad. Her cunning and shrewdness exemplified a unique form of capitalism and would have made envious the producer of even the most profitable pre-dawn infomercial.

With Mama conjuring spurious spirits and demons, Shred camped out in the living room in the corner and fed bits of rotting cheese to the rats behind the heating grates.

Leon, another young street dweller stopped by frequently to visit Mama and seek small jobs, while eventually bonding with Shred like a brother. Leon took to the streets in his early teens as a look-out for one of the area's renowned crack lords. The problem with Leon was that he was too well versed at his job, and quickly became known as the "kid with a dozen eyes" among the local dealers.

When Leon was working a job one night for his kingpin, he witnessed a shipment of presumably cocaine or heroin entering a competitor's warehouse. Leon notified his boss as to what he saw, who in turn, instructed Leon to leave the scene for the crew would arrive soon to scuttle the rival's delivery.

Leon more than happy to do a hand-off. He just stared through the rusty chain-links hoping to witness the showdown and feel the glory in knowing that he played a role in the home team victory.

Unfortunately for Leon, two of the rival's crew spotted him and approached him from behind. Leon heard the crunch of his pursuers' steps as they traipsed across the parking lot's inch thick layer of jug wine broken glass.

The boy spun around only to see the snarling rivals. Immediately, their hands claimed Leon's neck.

The next morning when the police finally found what was left of the young boy, they were relieved that they didn't need to call an ambulance.

Upon arrival, the first officer asked, "Hey Smitty, ya think we should call an ambulance? You wanna call it in?"

His partner slugged his coffee and responded, "Nah. Not necessary. I think I gotta zip-lock baggie in the trunk."

Shred regained his thoughts…

As the bubbles that were once Lu-Lu finally disappeared, Shred grabbed the binoculars and stared across again at the marina.

Now, it appeared that Justin and his daughter were being fed by whom Shred guessed was Justin's wife. Such a perfect American family, thought Shred.

He told himself that he would soon be back. He would return to claim what was by right, his cut. And the daughter upon which he gazed would provide the perfect bait for such an outing. The only problem was that Shred's vision of the little girl was mostly blocked by a large dock box and some heavy duty tackle, so he could not see her well enough to get a good description. All he could tell for sure was that these three sure looked like one big, happy family.

Chapter 14
Next Day— PSV Marina

"Hey Marl, Gerbil should be down any minute and Shark should be arriving in ten," Justin mentioned as he watched Marlene slice up fresh cantaloupe for Michonne. He still marveled at the maternal transformation that was engulfing the once oak-veneered former prosecutor.

Jus watched the activity at the end of the dock where there was a large members-only barbecue area. Every month for tax credits, the Dockmaster would lend the spot out to the local Bible Church so that they could hold prayer services.

They always seemed to be enjoying themselves at a level of excitement and fervor that was so foreign to Justin's empty soul. As they sang, chanted and greeted one another, Jus often looked on in amusement as it resembled to him a born-again mosh pit.

His thoughts returned.

"So, what's our answer gonna be, Marl? This is a great opportunity and I think it's one that's crucial to moving us forward."

Marl didn't look up as she sliced and diced. For a moment Jus envisioned his neck falling prey to the sharp tool in her skilled hands.

She finally turned to Jus, "Let's talk to Gerb and see what he thinks. That's if he's able to think, period. I dunno. I don't like it but if you two outvote me, I guess we can strategize how to make this work with as little risk as possible."

With that, the dock began to creak as it only did when the massive frame of Gerbil Turner would rumble down the gangway.

"What's happening, you silly kiddies in love?

"Anyone see my Lu-Lu with a Gerbil paw-print slapped on her ass? She's missing."

Marlene rolled her eyes, "No, Gerb. I can't keep track of the critters that escape from your zoo. If she's vanished, my guess is that it's by choice and that she's in a better place."

"Hey Gerb, did you take her out for a candlelight dinner last night?" asked a smirking Justin.

"Nah man, we stayed home and played Leapfrog. I kept losing."

The three gathered together around a small table on the dock, while Michonne gratefully took the bowl of freshly cut melon and said to Marlene, "You guys look all adult and busy. Can I go on the boat and watch TV?"

Marlene smiled and responded, "Of course, honey. Make yourself comfortable. We won't be long, and the clicker should be right next to the bed on the starboard side. Turn it on and press 524. That's the Food Network that you like."

Michonne took her breakfast and disappeared below deck. Jus marveled at what an amazing kid she was. The little girl was quickly adapting to the dockside lifestyle, and making herself at home and seaworthy after such an ordeal.

Marlene watched her go, "That kid is amazing. It's something that she loves those damn cooking shows. Funny…"

"Beats the friggin' Wiggles," said Jus as he turned to his partners and began the meeting.

"Alright guys. Gerb, Marl is privy to what I'm planning and I know that she filled you in on the phone last night. Curious as to your thoughts?"

Gerb rubbed his three-day stubbled face as if swimming in deep thought.

Marl silently grinned and thought that she smelled smoke.

Finally, Gerb responded, "Well, Jus. You know I'm not the shiniest coconut hanging off the palms, so I look to you to steer our rudder. I'm game for anything though, and if I can serve as security and make a few bucks, count me in. Also, while we're transporting these poor suckers who still believe in the American Dream, would you mind if, well you know, if I found myself a little foreign girlfriend? Ya know, someone exotic like in the movies? It's gets lonely at sea." Gerbil sported a mischievous grin.

Jus sighed, "No way, Gerb. Your prick is to stay in your pants and your hands are only for gripping an AK. We're not running some sex-slave operation, and your job is to have a scope trained on all of our passengers until we can dump 'em off."

As the three debated strategy, the fourth member of this new endeavor approached the Free Lance.

Captain Shark Bertolami gave Gerbil a bit of a start, and the security end of the team immediately went for the 9-millimeter tucked in his belt, but then heard the gruff voice of the seasoned captain.

"Hey, rodent man. Keep your hands by your sides and your eyes forward. Chill out. We haven't even had a chance to argue yet."

Gerbil stared at Shark and diffused the awkward greeting. Finally, he offered the captain a chair. While both played on the same team, they were famous for threatening one another with more than words and butter knives.

Jus was already losing patience.

"You boys done with the peacock strut? Let's get on with business."

Shark sat back in his chair, stared up at the mid-morning sun, and savored the shimmering rays as they warmed his salt crusted face. It was a long run back from Miami. While he was there to discuss the human ferry project with the PSV group, he also had decisions of his own to make regarding the proposed Conzalez mission.

As usual, Jus knew that he needed to establish order and assume control of the meeting. The typical dynamic was already at play, with Marlene patiently watching the boys verbally scuffle in the playground.

"Shark, Marl and I have discussed this at length, and while we both agree that we need to spread our wings in terms of our product offerings, she's especially concerned that this is unchartered water for all of us. How would you gage the level of risk?"

Shark once again looked up at the mid-morning sun as if to calm his racing mind.

"Jus, in the time that we've worked together, and I know it hasn't been long, but we've made solid money and I've never sent your vessel into the eye of a hurricane."

Jus nodded as Shark spoke.

"This venture could be extremely lucrative, and I guarantee that if we don't jump on it, then a half-dozen wanna-be pirates up and down the coast are going to lay claim to the action. Trust in that my contacts tell me that the facilitators in Freeport are looking for quiet reliability. Most of our competition are inept, or too damn drunk to be able to maintain order on a ship full of imports who are already paranoid and skittish about even booking passage. If we stay focused, professional and sober - that means you Gerbil - we can turn a solid score. Look at it like we're just taking out another charter. Although our guests for the afternoon will be held below deck courtesy of Mr. Gerbil's rifle."

Jus thought for a minute and spoke, "Hey crew, let's go aboard the boat and snag a bit more privacy. There are too many ears and eyes on these docks."

The group boarded the Free Lance and stepped down into the spacious salon which was to soon house almost two dozen refugees in tight quarters.

"Hey, I gotta drain the dragon," which was spoken with classic Gerbil grace.

Marlene responded, "Use the forward head in the main stateroom. The guest one is having an issue with the pump."

Jus interjected, "Hey Gerb, why don't you grab a shower while you're down there? You smell like an August low tide," snickered Jus.

"Marl, didn't we talk to him about hygiene during operations? Man, I miss Meyer every day, but today he would have been especially helpful to have onboard. We coulda strapped Gerb into that Olympic wheelchair and rolled him through the damn carwash. The guy reeks!"

Marl rolled her eyes, "Guys, let's focus here."

Gerbil grunted and went down below and was immediately met by a blast of frigid air. He didn't realize that Marl was a fiend about cranking the air conditioning unit. This also came much to the chagrin of Justin once Marlene became a permanent crew member.

Gerb could be heard screaming from below, "It's friggin' freezing down here! You should rename this tub the Mayflower. Does Ted Williams live down here? Maybe that freak Walt Disney?"

Justin shook his head as Shark asked, "Hey Jus, didn't Gerbil play football or something?"

Jus responded with an exhale, "Yeah. Didn't wear his helmet much, though."

This was followed by an explosive "Ahhhhh…" as Gerbil relieved himself in an animated fashion.

"Hey Marl," asked Shark, "You mentioned something about the head pump. It just dawned on me, how y'all gonna facilitate two dozen bathroom breaks?"

"With patience, Shark. Patience and careful monitoring."

"Yeah? You gonna trust that donkey with handling all that?" asked Shark referring to Gerbil.

"We'll make do, Shark. That's only one of several logistics items that make this job an especially risky venture in my eyes."

Marl hoped that Michonne did not hear this nonsense as she slumbered in the guest berth. She was grateful that the little girl would not be aboard for the trip.

As the group sat down and Gerbil finally emerged from below, the air in the salon immediately turned thick as they shifted back to business.

It was Jus who spoke first.

"Shark, before we get into the fine points, Marl and I are curious. In simple terms, what's your role and responsibility in this new endeavor?"

Shark leaned forward, "Basically crew, I will have no physical presence in the actual operation. I have my own new project outta Miami that I'm trying to plan as we speak. From what was described to me yesterday, my work is going to take me not too far from where you'll be operating. However, I wanna be clear that my goal is to never lay eyes on your vessel. All of the actual sweat work would be on you three and whoever else you want as support aboard the Lance. My cut from the deal is a fair finder's fee, and you'll be happy to know that it will be paid directly by the Freeport gang in Grand Bahama, and not out of your end. I'm merely a broker.

"I'll provide y'all with the Bahaman boat contact info, as well as the passenger manifest, which of course will be a list of bogus identities, but at least you'll have one to somehow keep track of who's who."

None of Shark's assurances seemed to calm a purse-lipped Marlene, yet Shark pretended not to notice and continued, "Overall, my job is to provide guidance, communication and instruction so that everything runs smooth and most importantly, safe."

The group was quiet in thought. Shark let a few seconds lapse and then continued while reaching into his bag,

"Here, Jus. This is a mini-EPIRB with a closed circuit that will let me know where your vessel is in case of an emergency, however it can't be traced by the Coast Guard. This little prick is black market, so please don't let Gerb eat it."

Justin nodded and took the device.

"Just keep it at the helm, and if for some reason you get into a jam, just throw this switch into the alerting position, and it will signal me as to your whereabouts. Please only use it in case you get in major trouble. If the tracker sounds off on my end, I'm gonna assume you're in a real fuckin' jam. Not sure how fast I'll be able to get to you, but I'll drop everything and blast. Hopefully, none of this will apply."

Jus nodded, "Okay, sounds good. How's our standing with the fearless and nosy marine authorities?"

Shark anticipated that concern, "My contacts within the Coast Guard, while few, are well greased by the Bahamans. The can't guarantee anything, but assured me that they would do everything on their end possible to make sure that you're ignored."

Marlene just stared at the sky in disbelief that they were about to agree to the mission.

"I'm not gonna jerk you guys around. This operation involves possible adversaries on and off the vessel. They key is to keep it immensely quiet as you're gonna be in open water with precious cargo. One that many would love to relieve you of.

"That's the Cliff Notes version." Shark ended his briefing and sat up straight.

Jus and Marl were clearly in thought and the air was heavy.

At which point Gerbil loudly farted and almost fell off the dock in acute pains of laughter.

Marl just rolled her eyes and foresaw an operation the likes that none of them had ever experienced.

Justin shook his head and turned to Shark, "Alright. So you have a new project and it looks like so do we. When do we start?"

To which Shark replied, "Like the song says, dawn's early light…"

Justin sat back and stared at a diving duck who had just snagged a small herring which he easily swallowed whole.

Chapter 15

Shark & Peeler aboard Booty Call

Shark carefully watched the sunrise. Life changed for him when he grasped the concept that while at first glance it may appear to have the usual appearance, upon a closer look, no two sunrises were the same. The angle, the hue, the intensity and the cloud patterns always differed. For Shark, that's where the vision of opportunity was found.

"Hey, Peel. Make sure the scuba tanks are full and that you got all the gear onboard. We're not goin' out there to play snorkel nice/nice like a coupla tourists. We're going hunting."

Peeler did not respond, nor did he have to. He and Shark had an exclusive form of silent communication when prepping for an assignment that at times involved being penalized by breaking the still air.

Shark was thinking about how he did not like Don Conzalez.

Yet, he trusted that the Cuban traficante de drogas would be good to his word and that success would render a substantial payment. An cash infusion that Shark could use as was pointed out as a jab by the Don during their meeting.

While he feared this assignment, it was the age-old belief in the score and an innate sense of greed that drove the seasoned captain to face many risky challenges head on.

The job that he was most happy to have thrust upon Jus' shoulders was the ferry gig about to be tackled by the Free Lance crew.

As Shark's thoughts bounced around in his head like a pinball, he caught a glimpse in the corner of his eye of Jillian slowly walking down the gangway toward the vessel. She wore a skin-tight plain white tank top with an overtly donned black bra, as well as soft pink sneakers with bright, white bottoms. Shark had informed her of his rule of no dark-soled shoes being allowed aboard the Call as to avoid pesky scuffs. She neglected to wear socks, and Shark fantasized that perhaps her panties had suffered the same fate of abandonment.

Shark thought to himself why did she need to wear Daisy Dukes on a friggin' treasure hunt? Great. More distractions for Peeler.

Jillian climbed aboard without asking for the customary permission, as she knew damned well that it was not required for this particular charter.

However, she politely greeted her two vessel mates for the next few days and said, "Captain, it's such a nice morning. Thanks for letting me book passage. Where would be an appropriate place to store my gear?"

Peeler had to swallow his quick answer to that, but Shark beat him to it with a more gentlemanly response.

"Welcome aboard, Ms. Jillian. Pardon the vessel's off-color moniker. If I remember correctly, it was Peeler who dubbed her and smashed the champagne across her bow."

Peeler proudly smiled wide.

"Anyway, we're happy to have you on this unique voyage and please feel free to stow all your belongings in the guest stateroom down below on the port side."

With that, Jillian disappeared into the salon while Captain Shark wished that she would stay there.

Shark fired up the blower and cranked the swollen engines, and as they found their footing, growled like Rottweilers at a burglar's leg stepping through a window.

When Shark's thoughts returned to reality, he barked, "Get ready, Peel! Throwing the lines in five."

And with that, Shark took control of his vessel and began to oversee one of the more challenging assignments of his long and storied career at sea. As he readied to blast off, he envisioned himself as the captain of a nuclear sub preparing for battle, "Hey, Peel! Flood tubes one and two!"

Chapter 16
PSV Marina

"Psst... Thud!"

Justin looked with satisfaction as his shot hit the top of a glass bottle fifty yards away. He and Michonne were at the far end of one of the docks which was just across from a burned out former part of the marina. During the previous winter, the place caught fire when some vagrants sought shelter for a few days and ended up torching a shed as they tried to stay warm. They scurried away before the authorities arrived, but they left behind several trinkets and cheap artifacts that served as target practice for Jus. He was now trying to teach Michonne some of his former craft.

"See honey, you hold the rifle steady. Here, lemme help you cause it's a little heavy."

With surprising ease, Michonne picked up and readied the powerful weapon.

"Then, just aim at the target and shoot. Here, look into the scope until the crosshairs are set on that old gray dish. It's closer and larger than my bottle, so it should be easier to hit especially with that scope.

"Aim carefully, and take your time. Take a deep breath and firmly hold the rifle."

Michonne loved the feel of the weapon in her hands. It was like a new mother cradling her baby for the first time. It smelled acrid from being fired, but also had a sweet scent from the oil that Jus had recently applied to clean the components.

The rifle of choice was a Remington 700 ADL Bolt-Action Rifle which was ergonomically pleasing for a young shooter. For accuracy, Justin swapped out the standard scope for a rare custom Leupold model. While Michonne appeared small at first glance, she was much stronger than Jus anticipated and was eager to shoot the target without any assistance.

"Okay, Michonne. Give it a whirl," coached Jus in as close to a fatherly gesture as he had ever exhibited.

POW!

Michonne's first shot went to the far right side of the plate and in the process nipped a few leaves and scattered some birds away from their front row seats.

"Try again, honey. This time aim a little more to your left. The most important thing to do is to concentrate and relax. Pretend that you're a hawk soaring in the sky who's looking down on a delicious, plump mouse."

Jus then realized that what he said might frighten a little girl, but he noticed that Michonne was not deterred and quickly found her zone.

Little did Michonne know, but she was being coached by one of deadliest snipers in the business, with a resume that included some high profile targets. Had she realized this, it would have only made her more eager to succeed.

BANG! SMASH!

The plate exploded and Michonne jumped in elation.

"See that, Justin! See that!"

"Great job, honey. We'll practice more later. I know that Marl is looking for you," Jus said as he noticed Marlene walking down the dock.

As she approached the two target shooters, she was still trying to formulate in her mind how she was going to explain to the child that she and Jus would be gone for a couple of days. Clearly the young girl and the older, surrogate mother had forged a unique bond.

"Michonne, honey. Justin and I need to go away for a couple of days but I promise that we'll be back as soon as possible. It's really important that you be a good girl and stay with Auntie Leslie aboard her sailboat. She brought it up from down south and lives onboard with her daughter, Avaline. You two will really hit it off and have a great time swimming and fishing and getting ice cream and…"

In a severe case of, it's a small world, neither Marlene nor Justin realized that Leslie was the ex-wife of a Gloucester commercial fisherman turned smuggler that Jus and Meyer robbed on the Boston North Shore over a year ago. She divorced the seafaring Captain Caleb Frost, took off with their daughter and headed down south to her wealthy family's Gulf Coastal homestead. Coming from money, Leslie had the luxury of being able to pay extra to have the divorce papers served to Caleb on Christmas Day. She was at least considerate enough to have the package wrapped with a red bow.

Shortly after, she borrowed one of daddy's live-aboard sailboats and headed off into the Gulf of Mexico, and eventually rounding the Florida Keys to try out a new life of freedom while home-schooling her daughter. Despite the unorthodox lifestyle, Avaline was a mature, intelligent and well-behaved girl.

Like everyone at PSV, Leslie was running from something, which in her case was an unfulfilling marriage to a oceangoing New Englander. Captain Caleb was hardly a bad guy, and did his best to dote on his wife and daughter, but Leslie grossly underestimated the culture shock of going from life as a privileged southern belle to a that of a Gloucester fisherman's wife.

Leslie and Marlene had become fast friends, but never clearly established the Boston connection, for rarely was any detailed truth spoken about one's past on the docks at Port Side Vow. It was an unwritten rule that was followed in a rather cult-like fashion.

Michonne was aghast. "No way am I staying here alone with strangers. I want to go with you! This is bull's balls!"

Marlene often marveled at the little girl's command of the vernacular.

"Honey, we need to go do something for our work. Auntie Leslie offered to have you stay with her and she has plenty of room. It's just her and Ava living aboard, so you'll be comfortable and safe. She's a kind southern belle with Dixie hospitality to match. You will be in the best of hands, and I guarantee that you and Avaline will be great friends within a day."

"She's not my aunt. Stop saying that!"

"Honey, it's just a term of endearment. No, she is not your true aunt, but she has offered to treat you like a niece and take care of you while Jus and I are out on assignment."

"What kind of assignment? Why can't I go?" asked a wide-eyed, curious Michonne.

"Well, dear. It's the type of assignment where children are not really allowed. It's kind of like going to see an R-rated movie. You know that it's only for adults."

The child rubbed her chin and looked squarely at Marlene, "Whaddya gonna take off your top and show your boobs?" at which Michonne belly-laughed as she was still in a giddy mood from having so much fun as a sharpshooter.

Marlene shook her head slowly with a slight smile, "No, honey. It's just that this trip is only for big people. Stay here and enjoy meeting new friends and having fun aboard that beautiful sailboat."

Michonne responded, "I hate sailboats. They're too damn slow."

Both were quiet for several seconds until Marlene asked, "Honey, I know that you've probably had a lot of people in your life walk away, and I'm sure that's been hard and has made you sad."

The little girl rubbed her neck with her right shoulder blade and remained expressionless until she said, "Marlene, I've moved a lot. I don't really remember much. It's strange though, cause I do remember when I was a tiny girl. My daddy was sitting in a chair. He was quiet, but he was nice to me, I think. I don't remember him as mean like some of the other people I had to stay with. But he was quiet and didn't say much. I don't think my daddy liked me."

Marlene noticed Michonne's throat gulp.

"Honey, I'm sure your daddy loved you. Maybe he was sick? Maybe he didn't know how to be a daddy? Maybe he didn't know how to love a little girl? I never met him, but I bet that today he's very sad that he wasn't a good daddy. But you know what? I'm sure that he's proud of you for being brave, strong and so smart."

"I dunno, Marlene. Why'd he run away? Why'd he leave a little girl all alone? I don't even really know if it's a real mem'ry or just a dream."

Marl breathed deep and looked at her, "Whatever it is honey, I'm here now. You can stay with me, and I promise I'll never go away and leave you. This little trip is only for a couple of days. Just know that I promise to come back."

Michonne was a little teary, but nodded again as a sign of agreement and understanding.

"I hope my daddy is proud."

Marl wanted to lighten the moment, "Heck, he'd be proud as punch if he knew you were already a plate-smashing sharpshooter!"

Michonne looked up and could almost touch her eyes with her wide grin.

Just then, Justin walked down the dock in an unusually slow pace. Marl was concerned, for Jus with the usual swagger of a former high-powered attorney and deadly assassin, was sporting the gait of a much older and weary man. Clearly, Jus was concerned about this new assignment.

"Marl, please see that Michonne gets set up and comfortable with those two. I know that Leslie said no, but give her a coupla hundred bucks for her expenses and time. She's really helping us out here, and I'm not certain as to when we'll be back. It's funny. Although she's only been at the marina for a short time, I swear that I know her name from somewhere. Anyway, please get Michonne settled. My mind is racing and I need to get the boat ready for shove-off. Let's try and throw the lines within the hour."

"Okay, babe. I'll bring her down now. Michonne, grab your stuff from down below."

Marl's instructions were interrupted by loud clomping that was testing the wooden boards' strength on the dock.

Jus and Marlene turned their attention from coaxing Michonne into a stay-cation on Leslie's sailboat, to the clod approaching them who happened to be their mission partner for the next two days. Gerbil had arrived.

He slung over his shoulder a large hockey bag, albeit this particular stowage did not carry provisions. God forbid he would think of a change of clothes or deodorant.

Instead he carted an array of automatic weapons that both Jus and Marl prayed (if they believed) would not be needed during their charter.

This particular hockey pack toted neither protective pads nor spare pucks.

His equipment was of a different type, and all Russian.

Present of course, was the customary AK-47, whose manufacturing began in the Soviet Union in 1946. It still shot the same 7.62x39 mm cartridge, and was as portable and lethal as ever. Gerbil often smiled at its versatility and resilient popularity among the world's terrorists and paramilitary groups.

He wanted to get a little funky for this gig, so where he was gong to be at sea, he brought along an ADS Amphibious Rifle. Also Russian made, but not until 2007, and shot a 5.45x39 mm cartridge with precise accuracy. The weapon's most important feature was that it did not mind getting wet.

With plenty of extra rounds stocked away in reserve, Gerbil showed up to play a naval version of full-court ball.

After Marlene returned from escorting Michonne to Leslie's boat, Jus fired up the Free Lance's twin CAT diesels. They didn't purr like kittens, but rather roared like their lion cousins, and it was the sheer torque, speed and fuel efficiency that Jus cherished for particularly challenging runs. He was used to a rendezvous to in order to pick up counterfeiting supplies, however this was to prove to be a new and more challenging form of contraband cargo.

"Hey Marl, get Rambo settled and then yell when you wanna throw the lines." barked the nervous captain who was embarking on his first foray into what felt like the modern day slave trade.

Marlene dutifully instructed Gerbil to chill out and showed him where his post would be once they finally had the guests onboard. Marl, who was always afraid of dehydration in the southern sun, took a swig of G-Zero and looked up at a cloud riddled sky. She paused and stared at the slowly meandering whips of white vapor. As they mutated with the wind, she swore to herself that she saw the shape of a unicorn, which was something that she had never witnessed during her South Boston childhood. Back then when she stared at the clouds in the sky, it was to only reveal the form of a devil or a serpent. Today, there was hope. Nervous hope.

Marlene tossed the lines, "Okay Jus. Your helm, Cap! We're loose and live."

Jus threw the starboard engine into reverse and slowly pulled away from the tight slip. The way that the marina was configured forced Jus to back into the channel, which he entered with two blasts from his horn.

Unbeknownst to Justin, right before shove off, there was a pair of feet tip-toeing down the dock right as he was about to slide the boat into gear.

Fortunately, there were no other vessels claiming the fast lane so Jus spun her in a circle hard to starboard and headed out to open water. Thus began a trip that would change everyone onboard.

As Jus passed the no-wake marker, he leaned on the throttle and gave her a bit of a goose in order to find a plane. The Cabo hull and finely synced CATs responded in tune, and the show was on.

As he glided her onto plane, he noticed to his port side a pod of dolphins frolicking among the small white-capped sea surface. Jus wondered what it must be like to not have any worries or responsibilities and just dance among the waves all day. The only concern being the occasional Great White, though as well documented, dolphins over the years had proven resourceful at keeping the big predators at bay.

Meanwhile, down below deck Gerbil was checking his gear and setting up shop. He would keep the AK-47 in his hands at all time, while the "water gun" as Gerbil dubbed the ADS Amphib, would remain slung over his shoulder and would only be used in a jam or if they ran into angry, turbulent seas. He still preferred the AK, for Gerb was old school and set in his ways to the extent that on occasion he could have written a twisted column for Yankee Magazine.

The afternoon's overcast sky served as an appropriate reflection of Justin's state of mind. He thought to himself how ironic that he, who for years had set up a rifle scope and removed targets' heads, was now afraid of giving a group of wandering souls a ferry ride.

He prepared on making the run well into the night and picked up his cellphone in order to contact Shark to make sure that the rendezvous vessel was on time and had the proper waypoint for their meeting place in the middle of the warm gulf stream.

Similar to when on a former Boston mission, Justin sat back in the helm chair and let the engines do their work, while he did what assassins do best. He waited.

Jus had thought of everything, and was aware of each aspect of every inch of the underway vessel. The piece of knowledge that the captain did not possess however, concerned a pint size stowaway who had hopped aboard just as they were pulling away from the dock, and who had stealthily wormed herself down belowdeck under the noses of the three preoccupied adults. She found a cozy little cubby under one of the guest stateroom berths. It served not only as a perfect hiding spot, but also as a comfortable place for a nap. As the calm seas gently rocked the large flybridge vessel, Michonne felt her eyes grow heavier with each passing wave.

Chapter 17

Aboard the vessel Booty Call

As Captain Shark slowly approached the piece of ocean marked by the waypoint that he was given by Don Conzalez, he gently dropped the engines' RPMs down so as to not overshoot his target.

Jillian was glowing on the bow in a lime green string bikini and bright lemon-yellow flip-flops. Peeler thought that she looked like a ice-cold can of Sprite whose sweetness he'd love to savor. He tried to concentrate and keep his thoughts occupied by checking and re-checking the dive gear that was critical in order to pull off a safe operation. All air tanks were full, regulator airwaves clear, and both masks were wiped clean of dust and salt.

Fortunately for the two divers, the seas were a hardwood floor and the sometimes feisty currents were peaceful due to a slack tide.

Jillian stared at the open ocean and admired it's beauty with a sense of gratitude. She knew that nothing was more alluring than a beckoning sea, which to her was so vital to her sanity and stability. Although she lived in a luxurious state, she'd trade it all tomorrow just to be able to melt into the waves and live the simple life of a mermaid about whom she dreamt as a child. The older she got, the less concerned she was with the cars, boats and waterfront condos. She was well aware that one could not take those things once the hourglass emptied, and in her mind she whispered to herself that old hackneyed query, "Ever see a hearse dragging a U-Haul?"

It was moments like these when she remembered her days growing up in the outskirts of Havana. Jillian was one of six siblings, and all of the rest all boys, so the little ramshackle house constantly radiated testosterone, while the sheets incessantly crunched.

Her father, Carlos, took off when Jillian had just turned three, so she had little if any memory of him. The way the story went was that he left the house one morning saying to her mother that he was going into the city to buy supplies for their little farm. In reality, he owed a local odds maker an overdue sum from losses on the local pit-bull fights, and he had to go before the gangster and beg for more time to pay. The meeting did not go well for Carlos as he was never seen again. Local lore tells the story that he ended up a permanent part of a small coral reef about six miles northeast of Havana Harbor, and became a popular curiosity for tourists and scuba enthusiasts.

Jillian's mom, Maria, was left with a house full of mouths to feed and also mouths that also loved to yell and argue. Jillian hated the noise and would often retreat to her corner and try and read a book. She adored reading and it became her escape. Even in the present day, Jillian often found her intellect overlooked. She was extremely well read with Hemingway being her favorite, having devoured The Sun Also Rises, The Snows of Kilimanjaro and The Old Man and the Sea, and she often viewed herself to be a modern-day version of the archetypal Code Hero having endured the cards that life had dealt her.

Maria wanted the best for her children and was desperate to secure for them a better future. She realized quickly after the disappearance of Carlos, that she would remain living and eventually dying on that little farm. She did not have enough land to make a living by merely growing crops, so she did what certain women in her village had already embraced. She took up the oldest profession in the world.

At first, she tried to keep it a secret by renting a room at a local inn as her place of business. However, this was short-lived after the innkeeper realized that he could command triple for what he was charging Maria due to the demand from some of the other local ladies of the trade.

Thus, Maria had to find a way to use her own modest bedroom as her occupational backdrop without letting her children know what was transpiring, which was impossible with a house full of teenage boys.

At first, Maria would only take clients late at night after the kids were in bed, but then the money started to roll solid and she saw the opportunity to quickly make some decent cash and to eventually find a way to get her kids to America where they could dream bigger dreams and realize loftier visions.

On her cot one night, Jillian was unable to sleep and heard her mom open the door and let someone in. She could not hear exactly what they were saying, but the voice opposite her mom's was clearly deep, confident and slurring.

A few moments later Jillian heard nothing.

Suddenly, she heard her mom shriek a scalding terror. Jillian blasted out of the space that she shared with two of her brothers and ripped open the door to her mother's bedroom. Maria was sitting up in the bed, but not exactly upright. She was rather propped to her right side, as her head dangled on her shoulder like a child's broken doll.

Her customer for the evening, who was clearly intoxicated and swaying in place, had become disenchanted with the services rendered and proceeded to break Maria's neck with his bare, burly hands, twisting it like one does a lobster tail.

Jillian screamed in horror at the ugly man and turned to run out of the house seconds before the murderer could grab her by the nightgown.

She ran and ran and didn't stop for twenty minutes.

It was then that a car pulled up whose passengers happened to notice the frenzied-looking little girl and felt pity.

It was a beautiful car and was not one normally found in the Havana outskirts.

Juan Conzalez stepped out of the vehicle and looked in shock and wonder at the young panicked girl before him. He was transfixed by how she resembled his own little girl who now slept with angels.

"Be still, child. Be still. Fear not from where you run," assured Conzalez, "You're safe now. C'mon in the car and get warm."

Conzalez barked at his driver to fetch a blanket from the trunk, and to wrap it around Jillian who was slowly crawling into the backseat.

It was then that Conzalez took in Jillian and from then on treated her like a princess. At first glance they may have appeared to have the markings of a lascivious situation, but Conzalez kept a deep secret that he only shared with the little girl at her Fiesta de Quinceanera.

Several years before as Conzalez was beginning to spread his business interests and center of influence over his small region of Cuba, he and a bodyguard rode into town one day to have what was supposed to be a routine meeting with a local hombre de influencia. Ostensibly so routine, that Conzalez brought along his young daughter, Munequita, so that she may enjoy the pretty ride through the country. He doted on the angelic young girl, and she looked up to her dad with the same eyes that gazed upon him at the moment of her birth. A once in a lifetime bond solidified by a quick glance that he expected would endure for eternity.

Conzalez, Munequita and Juan's bodyguard entered the quiet cafe and immediately sat down at a large table with Conzalez's meeting host, Patricio, who was escorted by a colleague, whose only discernible feature was a bronzed-over scar that ran from his right temple in a half-moon shape to his lower lip. At the sight of Munequita, Patricio looked a little unnerved, but maintained composure and decorum.

"Welcome, Senor Conzalez. It is kind of you to travel such distance to accept my lunch invitation. I see you have brought a colleague but more importantly, you were kind enough to bring along your lovely daughter to grace our presence," as Patricio glowed a warm, gentle smile toward the little girl.

"Little darling, I'm going to speak to your father in a form of Cubano that you might not understand, but please relax and enjoy this humble cafe. Some refreshments will be along shortly"

Conzalez and Patricio began their discussion as the best of friends by trading the traditional banter of stories and anecdotes in order to make one another smile and relax.

"Our life is good, senor," proudly spoke Patricio, "However my wife is still after me about how the kids do not show enough respect, and how the pumas keep eating our chickens." he said with an awkward cackle.

"Indeed," responded Conzalez, "But those are the fortunate problems of us simple farmers."

Quickly the host's tone changed and Conzalez realized that this meeting was suddenly donning an unexpected undertone.

"Senor Conzalez," Patricio cleared his throat, "It's with my utmost respect that before we discuss our intended matter, I would be remiss not to address a certain situation which occurred on Camino Pionero early last week."

Conzalez's eyes sharpened, and his look hardened.

"You see, a shipment that my men were bringing back from the Cojimar fishing docks never arrived at its intended destination, which in this case was my farm. Nor did any of my trusted amigos, Senor.

"While I am certainly not making any accusations, I must inquire as to your level of knowledge regarding that shipment.

It was witnessed by many neighbors that a few men in your loyal employ were seen in the area around the same time. You see, as a thinking man I cannot help but formulate certain conclusions, Senor Conzalez."

With that, the room's din of noise was inhaled by an open window.

Despite the tension, Munequita merely stared in wonder at Patricio's bodyguard. She fixated on his facial scar, and in a way admired its beauty. Its simplicity.

Patricio continued, "Please understand that I do realize in our business, we always run the risk of unfortunate occurrences. However, perhaps I am growing old and cynical, but I do not believe in coincidences."

Conzalez gently wiped his mouth with a napkin and placed it on the rough wooden table.

"Senor Patricio, I cannot say…"

Without the slightest warning, Patricio's associate stepped back from the table and drew a pistol. Conzalez quickly thrust his body over Munequita in order to protect her from the shots. Juan's bodyguard was killed instantly after being shot in the temple, and then the gunman turned to fire on Conzalez. While blocking Munequita, he took two shots to the upper back and shoulder. Within an instant, Patricio, his hitman and everyone else in the cafe ran and fled.

With pain surging through the top half of his body, Conzalez felt the intense confusion of shock, but then with adrenaline-surging arms he pushed himself off the ground to unveil Munequita who remained still on the cold, dusty, cement floor.

While Conzalez's first impulse might have normally been to touch his wounds and seek a mental inventory, instead his eyes blazed focus on the sea of crimson flowing from Munequita's contorted shape.

In a moment of unspeakable horror, he realized that the two assassin's bullets ripped clean through his body only to lodge themselves into the innocent Munequita, whose last living sight was the image of that perfect half-moon scar.

The cafe was still, and a songbird quieted.

Back to the present moment on Booty Call, Jillian gave her head a quick shake and returned from the depths of her vivid daydream. She had to focus on the mission. Conzalez was counting on her to be his eyes and ears for the duration of the crucial operation.

"Peeler!" shouted Shark, "Let's don the jester's motley and get our gear on. We're going fishing!"

And with that Peeler started grabbing tanks and BCs, while simultaneously counting dollar signs and lap dances in his salty air-filled head.

Chapter 18

Aboard the Free Lance

With relatively calm seas, Justin could easily maintain a stately cruising speed of twenty-two knots. Everything appeared under control, and Marlene and Gerbil were busy prepping the salon for how best to situate the soon to be arriving human cargo. It was then that Jus decided to check on his off-site partner, Captain Shark.

"Booty Call, Booty Call, this is the vessel Free Lance. Come in, Shark."

Justin waited for ten unanswered seconds and continued, "I repeat, Booty Call please come back to Free Lance." Justin and Shark had predetermined that they would communicate on an obscure channel as to avoid surveillance.

After a few seconds of static, the welcomed and familiar voice of the seasoned salt dog barked through Justin's speaker, "Free Lance this is Booty Call. How goes it there, Captain Jus?"

"Great to hear from ya, Shark. Yeah, things thus far are smooth as a baby's bottom. Very fortunate with these fair seas, and I trust you're seeing the same. We're making much better time than anticipated. Any chance that you can ask the rendezvous vessel to step on it and meet us at the waypoint a tad early? Over."

"No problem, Jus. I'll radio them now. Peel and I are about to hop in the drink and do a little treasure hunting. I'll hail the

Bahamans and if you don't hear back from me in five minutes, proceed with your current course and speed. If there's any snag, I'll let you know right away. Jus, when you do make physical contact with the Freeport vessel, keep all ears and eyes open, and the safeties flipped off all your weapons. I don't foresee any problem, but it's still the wild west out here."

Justin grunted in agreement, "That's a roger, Shark."

"Peeler and I will be underwater for about forty-five minutes, but our first mate Jillian will be monitoring this channel in case you run into a jam. If they're any concerns whatsoever, I can blast out there in less than an hour and offer any assistance. Just don't fire off that EPIRB signal unless you're really deep in the shit. Safe travels, and we'll be in touch in a bit. Booty Call, out."

Justin relaxed his tight shoulders knowing that not far away he had back-up in case any aspect of the project went awry.

Upon gathering his thoughts, he recalibrated both of the vessel's state of the art color, touch-screen Garmen GPS navigation units, and he also leaned another two hundred RPMs into the throttle.

Chapter 19
Shred's Hideout on Jekyll Island

Shred slowly lumbered and paced the cool cement floor of an old fishing shack that served as his headquarters. Back and forth he gazed at the half-dozen members of his gang of hoodlums. Shred felt that by divine right they were entitled to a slice of every illegal buck garnered on the South Georgia coast.

"Gentlemen, it's with both rage and embarrassment that I have learned of certain activity transacting right under our noses. In the midst of our eyes and ears, there appears to be an established and lucrative operation well underway."

Shred paused and picked up the long spear gun that he often used to shoot grouper, which also served as a handy walking stick for effect.

"You see, everyone within fifty miles of here knows that we own this slab of coastline, and proper tribute and respect must be paid by all who engage in certain types of commerce. Of course, we are not thieves. If a competitive enterprise is a failure, then we would not look for a cut. However, if one of our neighbors believes that they will enjoy healthy profits free of paying our proper protection tribute, then that is an inexcusable sign of disrespect. Rules must be followed, lest said regulations lose their teeth. Unfortunately, the next step is chaos."

Shred continued to pace in a Negan-like fashion, as beads of sweat began to appear on the foreheads of some of the gang.

"You see, when I was blessed with the vision as how to construct our well-oiled organization, I was firm in that I only wanted to hire the best. And I believe that's who we've gathered in this room."

The group collectively grunted and nodded to one another.

Shred continued in a stately manner, "I gave you each a territory to watch over, and to own responsibility so that you always feel like true partners and not hired deckhands.

"This particular operation that greatly concerns me appears to involve a rather profitable counterfeiting operation based out of Port Side Vow Marina. Now, I know what you're thinking, it's a bunch of washed up sea-dogs and two-bit weed runners. However, therein lies the genius of the strategy. Who the hell is going to pay attention to that land of misfit toys version of a boat yard?"

Shred suddenly turned and stared at his crew.

"However, one of you was supposed to have that location in his territory portfolio. I should have heard about this operation a long time ago from one of you! Not via second-hand last night from some nickel whore!"

The cabin's air thickened as the gang's nerves were awakened.

"So, it's time to man up! Whose responsibility was it? Speak right now, or risk being fed to the bull sharks at first light. I am not fucking around this time!"

Silence blanketed the room to the point where the only sound to be heard was the persistent heavy drop from a rusty sewer pipe.

To Shred's left he heard the faint voice of Squid Kruck, however he could not understand what the sea dog was saying.

"Speak up Squid, you puke!" shouted a quickly turning redfaced Shred.

Squid sat up, "I'm sorry boss. That's my assigned area. I just never paid it no mind as it was always so quiet and full of burnouts. I'll investigate right away."

Shred calmly replied, "No need for that now, Squid. You're gonna have other things going through your mind."

Suddenly Shred picked up the large spear gun and,

PSSSFFT!!

Shred fired a sharp-tipped three foot spear directly through the middle of Squid's forehead. The force was so strong that the spear went through his skull and impaled the hoodlum against the cabin's half-rotted walls.

The room remained still, as the other members of the crew stared straight ahead.

Shred barked, "Two of you clowns take that lazy piece of shit and go dump him beyond the reef with a chain necklace. The rest of us need to discuss how to infiltrate this self-proclaimed Shred-exempt counterfeiting operation."

Shred then tried to calm the air.

"I have a plan. It appears that our money-printers have a young daughter. I'm not sure how old, maybe early teens? I dunno. Anyway, during my second surveillance I couldn't get a great vantage point, but I noticed that the girl was now moving about on a nearby sailboat's deck. Our first course of action will be to relieve said sailboat of the young counterfeiter-in-training, which will provide us with an immediate hostage.

"We'll move when the time is right, but I don't want to wait too long. The main vessel seems to have disappeared from the dock. Most likely on a mission. A mission that in their current state of hubris, they think that they will not have to share the bounty. Selfish bastards."

And with that, the body of Squid Kruck was tugged off the wall and wrapped in thick anchor chain in preparation for a permanent underwater vacation.

Chapter 20

Aboard the Booty Call

SPLASH!...

Shark and Peeler both hit the warm Gulf Stream at the same time after jumping off the vessel's stern. They tangoed with their thoughts in wild anticipation, for Conzalez was convincing in what the treasure hunters might find.

They slowly let the air out of their BCs, and descended to a depth of about forty feet. Due to the clarity of the Stream, even at that depth one could still clearly see Booty Call's fiberglass hull bobbing on the soft waves.

Jillian remained on board as both look-out and radio monitor. She had a small device that could be used to signal Shark in case of an emergency on board. The dangerous beauty also kept close watch over several of the vessel's weapons which she could employ with complete skill and dexterity.

"How you doing over there, Peel?" Shark spoke into his regulator's remote microphone that served as the two hunters' means of communication while underwater.

"All clear, Skipper," responded Peeler in a loud, but crackled voice, who motioned over to Shark with the universal A-Okay hand signal.

Once the two divers reached the sea bed, they surveyed the terrain, and by instinct Shark selected a direction. With visions of blondes in bikinis and coladas in coconuts, Peeler swam twenty feet behind Shark's slowing waving fins.

Chapter 21
Port Side
Vow Marina

"Holy Shit! Where'd she go?" Leslie yelled to her daughter Avaline aboard their usually tranquil sailboat.

"She was supposed to stay aboard. Ava, did you check all the space below?"

Avaline rolled her eyes, "Yes, mom. There's no sign of her anywhere. Maybe she just went for a walk?"

Leslie knew damn well that Michonne had not simply wondered off on a leisurely dockside stroll. The little girl was told by Justin and more importantly, Marlene, to stay put and do as she was told by her babysitters while the couple were gone for a couple of days.

Avaline suggested, "Why don't I just call the police or the harbormaster?"

This was where Leslie was torn, for while she did not know exactly what Jus and Marl were up to, she knew that a police presence on the dock would not be well received by her neighbors who themselves could end up in hot water for engaging in various extra-curricular activities. Leslie liked and admired Jus and Marl, but she felt the vibe that they exuded painted them as risk-takers and rule-benders. While the vast majority of PSV members took some brazen chances with their various escapades, Lesie felt that Justin and Marlene might be borderline reckless.

She thought of running over to the next set of docks in order to bang on Rachetta's 42-foot Fountain Lightning speedboat dubbed The Grim Reaper. Rachetta had a twisted sense of humor, and her vessel's moniker stemmed from her occupation of twenty years.

Rachetta was a Hospice nurse for the Glynn County Visiting Nurses Association. Due to the nature of her profession, Rachetta prided herself on a long career characterized by adoring love bestowed upon her by her patients and their families, while so many others found it difficult to endure the occupation's emotional toll. And it was a deserved sentiment. Rachetta was one of the best at her craft, and was in high demand throughout the county.

While nursing and caring for the terminally sick was Rachetta's passion and calling, she also didn't mind the moonlighting aspects of the job. The fact remained that none of Rachetta's patients were ever going to get better, and though that saddened her at times, it did present a wonderful business opportunity for the industrious nurse.

Rachetta could almost guarantee her side-occupation clients multiple batches of unused and abandoned stashes of hard to obtain medications that held a handsome street value. At any time, if a client felt down or overly anxious, one could swing down to the dock, knock on the Reaper's cabin door and request a weekend's worth or Ativan or Xanax.

She was especially popular right after the holidays when the usual detoxers tried to kick off their New Year's resolutions. For those poor souls, it could be an ugly scene until Nurse Rachetta could provide the average addict with a healthy dose of shakes no more.

Rachetta stayed away from dealing in anything that began with the preface "Oxy", but pretty much anything else was fair game in her version of a much-needed and valued public service. Plus, her real patients were never going to miss those final doses, and were probably applauding her from up in Heaven for being so entrepreneurial. Such was the culture at Port Side Vow.

Leslie gathered her thoughts and realized that her neighbors were not the answer, nor was notifying the police just yet.

She relaxed and turned to her daughter, "Ava, I'll try and hail Justin on the radio, but my guess is that by now he's outta range. Let's just hope that the kid wandered up the street to play in the park, and that she'll be skipping down the dock any minute. I mean, she can't have much money on her, and she's gotta eat at some point."

Ava patted her mom's shoulder while Leslie tried the handheld VHF in order to hail Free Lance. While her head was in a whirlwind knowing that most likely Justin was too far away to be reached, she realized that she had to maintain control so as not to panic her daughter.

It was then that she thought about what her calm and collected ex-husband, Captain Caleb Frost, would execute as a strategy. Surely, he would instantly have a creative Plan B. During their sub-par marriage, he was the partner who could always maintain a sense of grace under pressure. She always figured that it must have had something to do with his being a Gloucester fisherman. These were the days when she missed him the most.

Chapter 22
Aboard the vessel Free Lance

Justin was nearing the agreed upon waypoint, and grunted as he stared intensely at the brightly lit radar screen.

"See anything yet?" asked Marlene.

"Yeah, something just showed up on the fringe of the range. Could be our Bahaman people movers, or it could very well be the Coast Guard who were tipped off and beat us to the scene."

Jus was in a focused zone, reminiscent of his days in Boston and the moments before he would pull the trigger on some unsuspecting target two hundred yards away. Marlene noticed the change in his look and disposition, as his vocabulary grew terse and his eyebrows lowered.

Justin felt fortunate that throughout the voyage they had encountered relatively fair winds and calm seas. Still, even by his standards as a former assassin, this mission was wrought with variables and danger. However, he seemed to relish operating from within the epicenter of the riskiest assignments.

"Marl, we're getting closer. You and Gerb go up on the bow and let me know when you get a visual of the vessel on the horizon. At least they're prompt if it's who I hope it is. Keep Gerbil focused, and make sure his hands remain on his AK and not your ass."

Marlene smirked and went to fetch their so-called "security officer".

"Oh, Justin," quipped Marlene, "I'm flattered that we are minutes away from what could be a life-changing project and you still fancy my ass. Perhaps Gerbil isn't as interested though?"

"Marl, Gerb would screw a wad of Silly Putty. Now post station on the bow and yell when you've got a visual."

Marl got a kick out of seeing Justin break a sweat.

He sat back in the captain's chair and kept a moderate speed headed straight for what he hoped would be the start of a lucrative new business line that would hopefully not involve removing skulls with long-distance rifles.

While nobody would dub him an addict, at the moment Jus was feeling the haunting cravings of a junkie holding a burning spoon.

All the while, Michonne remained hidden below in the guest stateroom. She was comforted by the fact that she was physically so close to Marlene. This relaxed her to the point where she was able to enjoy catching up on the kind of restful sleep that only the ocean's movement could provide.

Chapter 23

Port Side Vow Marina

"Mom, I'll go up and look for her. I'll bet you anything she's at the video game machines or the ice cream stand. She can't be too far. There aren't many attractions close by. She probably got bored on the boat, or is pouting that she had to be away from Marlene. She acts like Marl is her new mom. Don't worry, I'll take care of it. Can you spot me a few bucks so I can get us both an ice cream in order to bribe her to come back?"

"Fine, Ava. Here ya go," said Leslie as she forked over a twenty, "Be careful and don't be too long. We had better find her and in good spirits before our neighbors return. I gave them my word that I would keep an eye on the kid for a couple of days without her getting into mischief."

With that, Avaline hopped off of the sailing vessel and headed up the gangway in search of Michonne. It was not a big deal. She knew that the kid would eventually turn up, and she was in the mood for a Double Chocolate Chip in a waffle cone.

She reached the main landing of the marina and turned left at the restaurant which was currently closed for inventory, so the area was especially quiet. Almost eerie.

She reached the path that led thorough some bush area and ended up in the main parking lot. Ava felt a little frightened as she slowly walked through the path, for she had never seen it so devoid of human activity. She stopped to bend down to tie her sneaker and suddenly two large hands grabbed the backs of her shoulders.

"Don't you dare struggle, you little twit!" warned a fiery Shred, "Make one move and you won't be showing up at the next cheerleading practice."

Shred easily picked up the slim, teenage girl with his powerful arms, and threw her in the back of the van. Within seconds the vehicle whisked out of the near-empty parking lot and peeled out onto the main road.

Once back at Shred's hide-out cabin, Avaline was bound to a chair while being stared at by a group of men who resembled the Black Pearl's ghost crew in the Johnny Depp films. The dingy little house smelled damp and musty, and every corner displayed a varying shape of spider web. Scattered about the floor were empty beer cans and take-out chicken boxes. To young Ava, this was a place where even the filthiest, meanest wharf rats would shun.

After several minutes of watching her captors bang down several shots of rum, Shred sternly reminded Avaline to keep quiet or next would come the mouth gag.

"Here, drink this my little sweetheart. It will calm you down, jog your memory and hopefully loosen up your tongue," encouraged the now half-inebriated and increasingly dangerous gang leader.

It was all Ava could do to not vomit up the stale liquor, but she was in such shock that she barely felt the rum invade her tiny belly.

"Okay, Princess Bride. Tell me what your parents are up to. There's something going on at that little shit marina of yours and I want to know what it is. They're making money down there, and the word on the street is that business is booming. The only snag is that they're acting selfish and refuse to share."

Shred relaxed his shoulders and tone, "When you were a young girl, you were taught the importance of sharing, weren't you?"

Ava was beyond petrified, yet the alcohol was already beginning to dull her nerves.

"I-I guess so… Sir."

Shred roared back, "Knock it off with the Sir shit. You call me Captain. I am a fisherman and for the foreseeable future you are my bait. If at the conclusion of our time together, however long or brief, and you have performed to my complete satisfaction then I'll release you from the hook and send you back to swim with your ocean friends. On the other hand, if I am not totally happy with your level of cooperation, then I will drag you into the back-swamps and feed you to the fattest gator I can find. Feet first."

Avaline shuddered.

"Sir. No! I mean, Captain. I think that you have me confused with somebody else. I live alone on a sailboat with my mom. We lead a peaceful life and we're certainly not involved in any schemes to keep money from you. I mean…"

SMASH!!

Ava was startled by the explosion of crystals against the wall where Shred had given a glass ship's lantern the ol' Nolan Ryan fastball.

"Mind you, child," warned Shred, "I have no problem with using violence to get my way. Actually, I find it quite an efficient way to extract much-needed information as it always proves effective. Now, before you speak, think very carefully about what you're going to say. You're only going to get one shot. One. And it better be the truth or I will roll you in Elk blood before I cast you into the weeds. Now, speak carefully and tread lightly."

Ava was attempting to muster up all of the courage that she could, but with every passing moment, her will was evaporating.

"Captain, this is the truth. I live a simple life on a sailboat with my mom. We keep to ourselves and only have a few friends. We don't socialize. I don't even go to friggin school!"

That comment made Shred chuckle as she continued.

"There is this couple a few boats away who have a little girl staying with them who's a bit younger than me. I swear that she just arrived out of nowhere a few days ago. You must have me mistaken for her. She's been living with this couple, and I don't really know who they are or what they do. They're friendly enough, but mysterious and a little strange at times, just like the little girl who's not their real daughter."

Between the rum and the realization of the truth, Shred's demeanor softened as Ava explained the situation.

"The man and woman left on their boat several hours ago. I have no idea where they were going or what they're up to. Honest! All I know is that they asked my mom to look after the kid while they were at sea and now the little girl's gone missing. I walked up from the dock to try and find her. That's all. I swear!"

The room was quiet. Avaline wiped a tear and took a deep breath, "Captain, you're just a big bully. Your stupid ass kidnapped the wrong girl!"

Ava started to cry and Shred stepped back to let her weep. He looked around at his crew who stood still trying to look clueless, which did not require an Oscar-winning performance. Shred smiled to himself. He normally would never allow someone to insult his intelligence, but he admired the girl's bravery and her unfortunate accuracy.

Shred's gut instinct, which proved spot on the vast majority of the time, trusted Avaline's story. It made perfect and unfortunate sense. While he had seen a little girl on the dock, he now realized that this was not the same one.

Chapter 24

Aboard the Free Lance

Justin pulled back on the big diesels' throttles as Free Lance slowly approached the oncoming vessel. Minutes ago after Marlene had made visual contact, Jus radioed ahead to his Bahaman counterpart and via an encrypted exchange the two captains established one another's identity as partners for the day.

"Marl!" Jus yelled up to the bow, "We're tying up port to port. You stay up there and secure our bow line to her stern. Send Gerbil back here to secure our stern line to her bow. Tell him to keep his AK strapped on and ready at all times."

Though Justin's adrenaline was pumping, he was relaxed by the fact that the oncoming vessel was surprisingly newer, clean and impressive. Jus guessed a late model Hatteras, and from this distance he could see the captain's seemingly genuine happy smile. Jus guessed that the Bahaman was thrilled at the idea of his having his vessel finally free of its dangerous cargo.

The two boats made one another fast, and Jus walked on deck to greet the burly captain.

"Captain, thank you for being so prompt. I'm Justin, and I'm here to pick up some cargo that was arranged via our mutual friend, Captain Shark. Any of this ring a bell?"

The Bahaman made a slight chuckle.

"Ya, mon. I know who you are, Captain Justin. I'm Captain Thaddeus Bleechwooden from Freeport, originally from the island jewel of Jamaica. I'm known in these waters by the name of Bleach."

Jus chuckled a bit as he thought that the moniker was rather ironic.

Bleach smiled, "You laugh, mon. Yeah, everybody laugh, but I'm proud of my name. Back in Kingston dey call me 'dat cause me mother is Jamaican but me dah, eez from London. I'm called Bleach, but I'm the color of a rain cloud. Long story, mon. Let's get dis over wit."

Justin immediately liked Bleach's style, "Aye, aye, Captain. Please share your status report."

"Ok, mon. Captain Justin, I have fifteen guests aboard who seek passage for the second half of 'da trip to the U.S. Please trust that they have all been frisked by my crew and have been well-behaved during the first leg of the voyage. Many are a little seasick, but dey don complain much, mon. I'm confident that you will experience much the same. It was actually kind of a dull run, but fortunately everyone behaved and I don't really have anything crazy to share."

Jus realized it was going to be a little cramped down below, but readily replied, "If it's all the same Bleach, I'd like you to send over each passenger one at a time, and don't send the next one until you get my signal."

"Yeah, okay mon," responded an upbeat Bleach, who despite the uneventful trip, was eager to be relieved of his cargo.

Jus turned to his partners.

"Alright, guys. Gerb, go down below with your weapon ready and find a spot for each one to sit on the floor without blocking any doors. Keep the rifle visible and nimble to show them that you're not a novice when it comes to using it. Marl, you get the fun job of frisking these pilgrims as they come on board. I'll stay in the middle to help facilitate their trip below deck so they don't get any sudden ideas of getting lost in one of the state-rooms. All three of us need to keep making a mental headcount of the number of passengers at all times. Okay, let's get this done fast and smooth."

It took the passengers about two minutes each to hobble on board, be frisked by Marlene and then led by Justin down the salon steps. Many were having trouble walking due to the cramps and seasickness. Each would then be introduced to a piece of carpet by the intimidating Gerbil who would serve as their twisted version of Julie McCoy for the next several hours of the cruise.

Most of the passengers looked exhausted, but not in poor shape. Some appeared on the verge of tears from fear and nerves.

All except the last one.

Jus noticed the look in his eyes right away, and did not like the return glance. He could not tell the nationality of the last to board, but he clearly was not from County Cork. Not that Justin was a racist, but he was a contemporary of 9/11, the Paris concert attack and the horrors of Benghazi. Thus, he maintained a bit of the Arab-phobia that was part of the times, and aggregated by many within the collective unconscious.

"Marl. Make sure you pat that guy down a little extra," Justin said openly. At this point, he was not concerned if the guy understood English and was insulted. He was not alone in the mindset that the laws of political correctness did not apply once past five miles offshore.

Jus requested, "Captain Bleach. On your radio for a moment, please?"

A few seconds later, the Bahaman spoke, "Bleach, here. Come back."

"Hey Skip, this last guy to board. Did he behave himself during the crossing?"

"Ya, mon. I don like 'is eyes, but he kept to himself. I dunno, quiet."

"Okay, thanks Bleach. We'll be throwing the lines in a few minutes just as soon as I make sure my security detail has everything under control down below."

"No problem, mon. Take yer time. Bleach, standing by."

Justin went below and took inventory. Marl joined him as they surveyed the passengers who were their responsibility for the rest of the voyage.

Jus found Gerbil already fooling around and trying to flirt with one of the group who was clearly from somewhere in Asia.

"Hey, almond eyes. Love me long time?" asked the always unfiltered Gerb.

Justin was infuriated that Gerb was already acting like a caveman and was taking his eye off the ball, but Jus knew that he had to keep his cool and maintain stature. He had to instill in his passengers that everything was in perfect order and control, lest they see an opportunity for some sort of uprising.

"Officer Gerbil! Mind your station, and your friggin manners towards our passengers," Jus said calmly, but firmly. Gerbil got the hint and knocked it off.

This little incident reminded Jus of Marlene's warning that while Gerb was usually an operational asset, he could also prove to be the immature liability that could scuttle the whole mission. Unfortunately, he needed to be babysat as much as the passengers.

Gerbil immediately made a point of casting an intimidating presence with not only the AK-47, but also his fiery, crazed eyes.

Justin addressed the group, "You'll sit still for the next several hours. You will not speak. You will not get up. If you need to use the head, you will go one at a time and leave the door open. You will be monitored at all times by Marlene, who is also fully armed and dangerous. Bottled water will be provided. For those of you who don't understand English, you'll figure it all out as we go. Basically, just sit tight and behave. The seas are fair, so hopefully the remainder of your passage will be pleasant and without incident."

It was then that Jus noticed another nasty glare from the last passenger to board Free Lance, which made him uneasy.

"Hey you," yelled Jus, "Do you understand English? What's your name? Where you from?"

In solid English, the terse response was, "My name is Khalil."

And that's all that Jus would get for the moment, as the passenger did not volunteer another word or facial expression.

"Very well, Khalil. Smile a little, will ya? This is your lucky day. Get comfortable. Could be a long ride if we run into choppy seas.

Jus instructed Gerb and Marl, "Guys, you two stay below and watch these guys while I fire this girl up and shove off."

Gerb chimed in, "Hey Khalil, aboard this ship, I'm gonna call you, Tak."

Jus just shook his head and exhaled. He then quickly thought that it could have been his imagination, but he swore that he noticed a similar "Khalil-like" glower on one of the other male passengers who up until now had gone undetected.

For the moment, he chose to ignore it as he thought that he might be getting paranoid. Captain Bleach appeared to have experienced no problems.

Sifting through many thoughts, Justin walked up to the bridge and prepared the Free Lance for high-speed, open water travel.

During all of the commotion, Michonne had woken up in the guest stateroom. She yawned a few times, but made a point to remain quiet. She was worried that Marlene would be angry at her for sneaking aboard.

In the meantime, the little girl made herself comfortable. She was confident that if she felt like a refreshment, that she could sneak undetected a few feet across the stateroom carpet to the mini-fridge which held fresh water and snacks.

Chapter 25
Fifty feet below Booty Call

While Shark had his reservations regarding his current assignment, one thing for certain was that he was enjoying a kaleidoscope of a scuba outing courtesy of the Conzalez Family purse.

Peeler spoke into his microphone, "See anything, Skipper? While it's all pretty and whatever, we didn't come here to film the parrotfish eating coral."

"I know, Peel," responded an eye-roving Shark. "We're in the area. It's calm at the moment, but the currents out here can get feisty and move shit around. Be patient."

Suddenly, a large Barracuda made his presence known two inches in front of Peeler's mask, while baring a Ginsu set of teeth. He didn't lunge, but merely floated as if in mid-air.

Peeler realized that he'd been an idiot and had forgotten to remove his shiny anchor pendant prior to diving in predator-infested waters. He slowly removed the trinket, and stuffed it into his chicken wetsuit.

With the gleaming object now hidden, the barracuda ultimately lost interest and moved on, which Peeler considered an insult.

Shark suddenly yelled, "Peel, look! About thirty yards away at eleven o'clock."

The two treasure hunters quickly kicked their flippers into high gear. When they arrived at the spot that Shark had noticed, they feasted their eyes in awe, for before them strewn about in powder-thin sand were packages of what Shark intuitively knew was their pay dirt.

As Shark and Peeler surveyed the spoils, they marveled at the unique way each package was so tightly wrapped and bound. It was no mystery to Shark why Conzalez knew that this would not be a waste of time.

"Peel, mark this spot on your GPS. We'll head back, swap out for fresh tanks, and re-anchor the boat right here."

"Aye, Skip. Holy cow, look at all that shit! That's a lotta dope!" exclaimed an excited Peeler as he surveyed the ocean bottom landscape.

Shark instructed, "Before we go, let's each of us load up our bags with as much as we can carry on this first trip. We'll throw it onboard and get a close peek at what we're really looking at. My gut tells me that we won't be disappointed. Stuff as much as you can, and I'll do the same. It'll only take a few minutes."

Peel loved the sound of that. Almost as much as he loved the vision of his possibilities with Jillian once she knew that he was now a wealthy, successful treasure hunter.

When the duo reached the surface, their hired babysitter helped to get their gear onto the boat. As she bent over the starboard gunnel, the site of Jillian distracted Peeler's attention. He quickly thought of dull baseball to get back on track.

Jillian was curious and tried to peek at what the divers were bringing up, "You boys look happy. Any luck?"

"I'll show you in a few minutes, m'dear," said Shark who did not want to appear over anxious.

Once aboard, Peel spoke up, "Let's cut one open, Skip. Y'know, see what we got."

Shark pulled out his shin knife and removed one of the brick-shaped objects from his diving bag. He stuck the sharp blade into the thick plastic and sliced through several layers of tape and waterproof casing.

After he cut through and peeled apart the two sides of the three-inch incision, his hopes were proven to be true. With a dab of his finger, he sampled a quick taste of some of the finest cocaine that had ever hit his discerning tongue. He was grateful that it was not fifteen years ago, for back then the Booty Call would have skipped the westward trip home. Instead, Shark would have thrown the hammer down to speed off in a southerly direction to find whichever island was hosting the largest and most decadent party in the Caribbean.

"Shit, Peeler! We hit it, brother. We really hit it this time. This is gonna be one Hell of a score!" said Shark who is never easily impressed or excitable.

Peel's smile suddenly dulled as he finally realized the enormity of the project ahead, "Skip, this could take a while. Let's think about this. Why don't we take a break for a sandwich for you, and a coupla Kaliks for yours truly? Then, let's go after it."

"Not a bad idea, Peel. I want to get on the radio and make sure that things are running smooth for Justin. And hey! No sampling that shit!"

Peeler nodded as Shark approached the helm.

"Free Lance, Free Lance, this is the vessel Booty Call, over."

The air was silent for several seconds, until Shark repeated the communication.

Suddenly, the speaker spilled out the voice of Justin McGee.

"Booty Call, this is the motor vessel Free Lance. Hey Shark, I read you loud and clear. How goes your project? Over."

"We're doing well and ahead of schedule. However, I think that our efforts here are going to be a bit more time consuming than originally planned. More importantly, how are you faring and is the cargo in good order? Over."

The two captains began to speak in semi-code, which they both knew was a little overkill due to the obscure channel that they were monitoring.

Jus responded, "So far, so good, Shark. Things are calm like today's ocean, but my gut tells me that I need to keep a very watchful eye out for any sort of atmospheric disturbances. Over."

"Alright, man. Just hang in there. You have a capable crew, fortunately, and at least one of them has her mental faculties. Just shout if you need anything. Peel and I are going to take a little break before we begin the hard work. If for some reason you hail us and Peel and I are underwater, feel free to chat openly with our first mate, Jillian. You can't miss her with the sultry voice and Spanish accent. Over."

"Will do, Shark. Be safe out there. Lotta sharks in and out of the water. Will catch up later. Free Lance, over and out."

With Justin's parting words, Shark clipped the VHF's microphone and walked back to the vessel's cockpit.

"Hey Jillian, do you think that you can keep Peeler company for a bit? He doesn't bite, and if he starts to annoy you, either just give him more beer or stick him with a harpoon."

"If I must, Captain Shark. The problem is that I fear he might like it," responded Jillian with a chuckle.

"Peel, I'm going down below for a quick nap. I'm exhausted from the past couple of days. I'm not getting any younger, and I'm gonna need every bit of octane that I can muster to get this barn raised. In the meantime, keep your hands off both the control panel and our babysitter."

Shark took a three hundred sixty degree view of the area surrounding Booty Call. He sported a teenage grin followed by a snicker, and proceeded below deck. So far, the operation was going exceptionally smooth considering the size and scope of the project. Almost too smooth for the always wary Captain Shark.

Chapter 26
Shred's Hideout

Shred paced the floor. His head was heavy with troubled thoughts and potential outcome scenarios. Granted, Shred was a hardened, career criminal, yet kidnapping little girls was not exactly his bailiwick. He summoned Carty, one of his right-hand goons.

"Hey Carts, c'mere for a minute."

Shred's lieutenant meandered over with knuckles dragging.

"What up, boss? Getting to be a drag with this whiny kid hanging around."

"Shut up, you zombie. She stays as long as I say so. Forget her for a minute. I've been playing this game a long time, and my gut is rarely wrong. I should have been a friggin' stockbroker or a safecracker but it's a little late for that."

Carty blankly stared ahead like a sand eel.

"For argument sake, let's just say that the girl is telling the truth about the couple on the dock, her mother, the other kid, et cetera. And to be frank, I have every reason to believe that she is. If that's the case, what the fuck is going on down on that dock, and who is either funding or protecting the happy couple and their operation? They can't be working naked, or else they'd be in a crab trap getting their eyeballs pecked out by now."

As always, it took Carty a moment to respond as the synapses in his brain rarely fired on the first strike. The twenty-year marriage of Mary Jane and Old Thompson had taken their toll.

"I dunno, boss."

"Shocker," muttered Shred.

Suddenly, Carty had a rare thought, "But boss, I'll say this. Since we've been doing some recon on the joint, I have noticed this friggin' big dude going down to the docks a few times. He doesn't look like a boater and just doesn't fit in right. He's gotta be there for another reason. I know it."

"Ok, Carts. Black dude, white dude?"

"Boss, he's all redneck, and a lot of it. The funny thing is that I know that guy from somewhere. Can't place it at the moment, y'know my mem'ry ain't so good no more, but I seen him around somewhere. He had a bit of a funny walk, too."

"Whaddya mean, funny walk?" asked Shred.

"You know, boss. Kinda like Billy McMurtry had after you got mad and clipped off his four left toes. He could still walk, but it was a little strange."

Shred smiled, "Yeah, good old Murt. Dumb-ass Mick. He never was the same on the end of a diving board…"

Carty thought for a moment, and then light dawned.

"Wait, wait. I seen that guy a few times over at the Busy Beaver. You know, that titty shack about ten miles west of here. Yeah, I seen him there a few times throwing a lotta money around the talent. He seems to really be into anything that moves, but who isn't a white chick."

Shred thought for a moment, and then came to a realization.

"Damn! That's how Lu-Lu got her information. She was probably banging that oaf when he started telling tales. She fucked it right outta him! Hmm. Gotta give her credit…"

In some perverse way, Shred was proud of Lu Lu's intel-gathering acumen.

"Carty, I bet that guy's involved in this. Maybe as some sort of muscle? I'd bet my left one that this little brat here is telling the truth. We can't let her go though, or else we'll have a cop raid on our hands. Go tell the guys to make her comfortable and give her something to eat. There might be some old pizza in the fridge. Stay away from the grey slices. Unlucky day for her, but she'll have to sit tight for a while. Throw the TV on and give her the clicker.

"Meanwhile, I guess that all we can do is get back down to that dock and wait for the return of that friggin' boat. We'll bring kid with us as a little insurance coverage."

Chapter 27

Aboard the Free Lance

The calm seas slowly turned into small, northwest rollers. Jus tweaked his course so that the Free Lance took them at around 330 degrees on her compass.

Justin sat calmly at the helm and scanned his dials. Oil pressure was fine. Temperature was behaving, and the fuel gauges still boasted plenty of juice. He hoped for an uneventful passage and a clean drop-off.

Marlene and Gerb were down below with the cargo. While she was not brandishing her weapon at the moment, Marl had made a point earlier to show the group that she was keeping a Glock handy in her waistband. As instructed, Gerbil held the AK clearly visible in his hands at all times. While he was not pointing it at anyone, the passengers knew that one twitch and he could send a volley of automatic fire in their direction.

The majority of the group looked a combination of bored and seasick. To Gerbil, his only concerns were Tak and one that in his head, he had dubbed Tak, Jr. He had a similar set of eyes and that same creepy stare.

While Gerb was trying hard to behave, he was getting bored and a tad seasick, so he decided that he could use a distraction of sorts.

"Hey, Tak. Whaddya do for fun over there in sand land?

Gonna be a lot different in The States. No camel screwin' at night," chuckled Gerbil.

Both Khalil and Marlene gave Gerbil dirty looks until Marlene spoke firmly, but calmly, "Gerbil, let's all focus on the task at hand."

"Oh, c'mon Mother Hen. We're giving these poor slobs the gift of a lifetime. Hey Tak, how soon until you go on welfare? After that you can focus on blowing up children and Christmas shoppers at a mall? Or maybe dismember dozens of bystanders at one of our sporting events like those cowards did up in Boston during the Marathon. Real fucking soldiers."

Marlene put her hand in the air, "Gerb, just stop being an asshole and trying to bait them. Just leave everyone alone!"

Gerb shook his head, "Whaddya want me to do, Marl? Hand them each a bag of peanuts and the latest issue of Conde Nast?"

Khalil was turning red, and Tak Jr. didn't look much happier. Marlene was starting to fear that they had made a huge mistake in thinking that they could contain Gerbil's psychosis.

All Marl could muster was, "Gerb, please."

While she was trying to prevent this simmer to reaching a boil, the rest of the group merely sat and stared. They were equally as afraid of what might transpire, because for most of them their only interest was getting off of the floating zoo and onto American soil and hopefully a better life. They had risked, lost and spent everything they had for this one window of opportunity.

However, for the moment, Gerb was enjoying the distraction.

Khalil muttered something under his breath which Gerbil could not hear and only baited his gun-toting demeanor.

Marl's fear was growing and she yelled up to the helm.

"Justin! You might want to come down here."

"What now?" Jus muttered to himself as he threw the boat into neutral, and then descended into the cabin. Immediately, he glanced at Marlene who nodded disapprovingly over toward their rifle-toting security officer.

Jus barked, "Gerb, what the fuck are you up to? We only have a few more hours to go. Knock the shit off and find another activity."

"Jus, whaddya want me to do? It's boring down here and I'm gettin' seasick. I'm just passing the time and my audience here is enjoying my act. Ain't ya, folks? Course, most of 'em don't speakah any Eeengleesh," chuckled an amused Gerbil.

"Gerb, I'm not gonna warn you again. Be courteous to the passengers, or I'm letting you off at the next jagged reef."

Justin turned and walked back up to the helm. This was not good. He cursed himself for trusting the fact that Gerbil could maintain even a modicum of maturity and order.

While the vibe in the salon was starting to percolate, Michonne remained comfortable in her stateroom hiding spot. She found plenty of refreshments in the mini-fridge, and was enjoying the vessel's gentle rocking. She felt that she should go above to the salon, especially if for some reason Marlene was having any trouble, but her instinct told her that by doing so might cause more of a stir than be of assistance. She loved Marlene and was grateful for all that she had done. She also realized that at the moment it might be more helpful if she remained hidden.

Meanwhile, Justin realized that he might be smart by taking out an insurance policy. He grabbed the radio.

"Booty Call, Booty Call. This is the vessel Free Lance. Come in Shark."

After a few seconds, his radio crackled with Peeler's voice.

"Free Lance, Free Lance, this is Booty Call. Over."

"Hey Peel, is Shark around? It's nothing urgent, but I wanted to run something by you guys. Over."

"Jus, he just bunked down for an hour. We have a huge project ahead of us and he wanted to have all his steam. I can wake him if you want? Over."

Jus tapped his fingers on his jaw, as jitters were foreign to him.

"Nah, Peel. Let him rest. But do me a favor. I'm gonna hail you guys every thirty minutes for the rest of the trip and update you on our location and progress."

Jus recited their current latitude and longitude position, as well as their speed and course direction. Peeler wrote the coordinates down and confirmed receipt.

"Peel, I know this is a pain in the ass, but it's in everyone's best interest. Also, periodically I'll text you our position and heading, so you'll be able to track us without having to write it down. If for some reason you don't hear from me, even just a quick hello, all is cool, then please come looking for us. Please trust that I realize you're busy and don't wanna have to do that. Over."

Peeler responded, "Not a problem, Jus. Whatever you say. I'm not sure that Shark is gonna wanna leave our spot, but I'll let him know when he wakes up. Booty Call, out."

Peeler looked at Jillian for the first time without a lustful eye.

"Miss Jillian, it looks like we have a little side project to tend to. Do you mind answering the radio later while we're under water?"

"No problem, as long as you keep focusing on the task at hand. It will give me something to do aside from getting a rash from your constant jackal stares." responded Jillian.

Her comment did not embarrass Peeler. He was flattered that she noticed his interest.

Meanwhile, below deck in the bunk area, Shark had quickly fallen asleep and was unaware of the exchange ensuing above him. His mind painted vivid dreams of all of the dope that he and Peel were going to grab in a couple of hours, and the untold riches that it would provide. He was getting too old for the pirate life, and couldn't wait to exist on his own terms. While he didn't dream of sitting dockside all day, smoking a pipe and telling Perfect Storm sea stories, he did yearn to do what he wanted to do, when he wanted to do it. This was truly once in a lifetime type of stuff, and nobody was going to get in his way.

He envisioned Peeler bouncing from island to island like a Caribbean pinball, while constantly needing bail money and VD shots. Jealous boyfriends would have as many contracts out on him as there were jerk joints in Jamaica. Shark dreamed of a different path. He conjured up images of a simple existence in a place like St. Kitts or Nevis. Maybe start a little business teaching people how to scuba and spearfish? Whatever it would ultimately look like, he knew that it would not involve violence or risky illegal activities. He had satisfied his lifetime deductible.

And with that mind-dream thought, Shark rolled onto his other side and peacefully uttered a soft grunt of satisfaction.

Chapter 28

Onboard the vessel Free Lance

For now, all was quiet aboard his vessel, but Justin remained on high-alert. The wind shifted so he increased the vessel's speed in order to better greet the growing rollers to his starboard bow. The boat was shrugging off the bumps as he took them from the two o'clock direction. He could still squeeze out a few more knots per hour without getting everyone sick, while also closing the gap between the boat and the Georgia coastline.

At the stipulated time, Jus picked up the microphone.

"Booty Call, this is Free Lance. Come back, Peeler."

Peeler's voice responded after a few seconds, "Loud and clear, Free Lance. What's your status? Over."

"Fortunately, all's well Peel." Jus repeated his position, course heading and new speed. "We picked up a little bounce on the rollers, but nothing major and none are wearing caps. Talk to you in thirty. Free Lance, out."

Jus felt a sense of security that he was now in constant contact with Shark's vessel, and the activity down below seemed to have quelled.

Little did Jus realize over the diesel noise was that Gerb was still enjoying verbal potshots at Khalil every few minutes. Marlene was desperately trying to diffuse the situation without drawing too much attention. She knew that showing any sign of dissension or weakness could easily incite chaos in a matter of seconds.

Gerb continued, "Tak, every time you talk, you just whisper. I can't hear a damned thing you're saying and my hearin' is perfect despite a few gridiron concussions over the years. Man, I did get my bell rung a few times, come to think of it. Yeah… Shit, man."

Khalil was silent, but finally responded, "I need toilet. Need a toilet, now."

Marl and Gerbil exchanged glances.

So far on the voyage, nobody had requested use of the vessel's head. Marlene figured that it had to be due to dehydration and fear, but she was concerned that the first customer was to be the passenger who Gerbil was periodically peppering with annoying harassment.

Gerb finally spoke, but in a more sober, wary tone.

"Ok, bud. I'll take ya. But leave the door open and be quick with whatever you gotta…"

Marl interrupted, "Gerb. The pump's been acting up in guest head. He'll need to use the one in the main stateroom. I can take him."

"No, Marl, Stay here. I better do it. Show your weapon to let those with no English realize they're still being watched."

Gerb turned to Khalil, "On your feet. We gotta go down a few steps and then down the hall. Real slow."

Gerb quickly perused his rifle and made sure that Khalil saw the safety being disengaged on his automatic weapon. That did not appear to faze him, as he stood up, stretched his arms wide and yawned. He then motioned to Gerb as if to ask permission to proceed.

Gerb pointed with a head twitch. "G'head."

With Gerbil a few feet behind, Khalil stepped over the legs of his fellow passengers and walked down a few steps to the lower level. Gerb wanted to stay close, but also knew that he needed to leave a little room for mobility if the situation deteriorated.

Meanwhile in the guest stateroom, Michonne sensed movement and froze in her hiding place. She could hear Gerbil's muffled voice, and his tone immediately alerted her that something important was going on, for the big man was usually joking and goofing around. Her instincts told her to remain out of sight.

As they entered Jus' stateroom, Gerb reminded Khalil, "Hey, Tak. Leave the door open and make it fast."

"Hey Marl!" Gerb hollered up to the salon, "How's everything up there?"

Marl calmly replied in a semi-shout due to the diesel hum, "All is fine, Gerb. Just let 'em do what he's gotta do, and get back up here."

Meanwhile, Justin heard the din of moderate commotion, "Hey Marl, everything cool down there?" Instinctively, Marlene turned her heard toward the sound of Justin's voice.

That's all that Khalil's comrade needed to see. He had remained quiet and still during the whole exchange, but when he saw his moment, he shot up like a gazelle and tackled Marlene, while gripping a vice-lock hand on her pistol. Marl fell backwards hard against and end table with Tak, Jr. on top.

The sudden noise startled Gerb who jerked his head and was met with a lightning martial arts strike from Khalil, who then rammed the butt of Gerbil's AK into his right temple with jarring powerful force. For somebody so wiry and awkwardly dressed for combat, Khalil struck like a cobra.

Gerbil's hand met his stinging head, and in a stunned state he intuitively took physical inventory. That split second was ample time for Khalil to snatch the weapon out of Gerbil's hand and immediately turn the table on the situation. Within a matter of seconds, control of the lower level of the vessel had been relinquished to the two passengers, who were well acclimated to using brute force.

In the guest stateroom, Michonne heard the ruckus and her pulse was surging, but she dared not move. When she heard the cry of pain as Marlene was pounced on by Tak Jr., she winced as if getting a tetanus shot.

"Madide! You got her down?" asked Khalil with a shout.

"All set, Khalil," responded the cohort from the salon, who suddenly commanded English like an Oxford grad student. He had quickly applied a strong arm lock that rendered Marlene face down on the carpet, yet seemingly unharmed.

Justin, upon throwing the Lance into neutral, ran down the steps with gun in hand, but slowly lowered the weapon upon seeing Marlene's own Glock being held to the back of her skull.

Khalil led Gerbil down the corridor past Michonne's hiding place, and up the steps to the salon. "Go sit next to the woman." He then turned to Justin, " Captain, you join them."

Justin slowly sat cross-legged on the floor next to his lover.

"If any of you so much as twitch, Madide will blow a hole through the woman's head, which might even be powerful enough to pierce the hull of the boat. Remember, you idiots are convinced that we don't care if we die."

"She can't move, Khalil," assured Madide.

Khalil continued with crazed eyes. "Foolish and arrogant. Captain, I don't want to die, for I'd much prefer to live a long life aboard this fine vessel, and let you and your goon friend here warm up the seventy-two virgins for me."

Justin stared into Khalil's eyes as he formerly did into a rifle scope. For a split second, Khalil actually felt a slight shudder, to which he was not accustomed. He quickly realized that Justin might prove to be a formidable adversary.

Justin spoke up, "What he Hell is the point of all this? We're just giving you a lift. All your pals sitting here are looking forward to safe passage." he said with intended sarcasm.

"Captain, these people are neither my friends nor my concern. They know of us, and know to sit still and keep their mouths shut. Here's the deal. If you and your two friends behave, then the three of you, as well as the passengers will be let off at the nearest island unharmed. What you do from there is irrelevant. You will of course be relieved of all tools and communication devices, but you will at least have a chance to hail a passing ship. You are fortunate, for many of the more dedicated colleagues within our organization would just start slitting throats this very minute, but despite what you inaccurately perceive, we're not simply murderers. However, in the end if you all perish of starvation, alas that is Allah's will."

Justin kept silent and air grew heavier as Khalil continued.

"So, for the moment sit tight. Madide, keep your weapon buried in the woman's hair with the safety off. I need to phone our contact in order to coordinate a proper rendezvous."

Khalil had managed to smuggle a cell phone onto the boat despite being frisked. His loose baggy clothing provided numerous hiding spots which had proven effective many times before.

Justin loudly cleared his throat, "Well Khalil, it sounds like your plan is to leave us on a island with no resources. Then, you and Madide, as he seems to be called, proceed to steal my boat. Now, I would be remiss as a ship's Captain if I did not ask what are your intentions for my fiberglass daughter on your sick version of prom night?"

Khalil responded with a serpent's eyes and grin, "Captain, let's just say that your vessel's autopilot will come in handy during our operation. And getting your crew and passengers off of the boat will increase storage space and make for more efficient fuel consumption. She has a large fuel capacity, does she not? And she seems to have quite a bit of room for storing anything I might fancy."

Jus now stared at Khalil with an assassin's eyes.

"The beauty of this boat is that while spacious and rather fast for its size, it is not a boat that would draw unnecessary attention in these waters. She's perfect for our mission, and you will be most proud of her. My guess is that you are some kind of drug smuggler, for this is the perfect vessel."

Justin now understood where this was going, and it frightened him to the core. During the tense dialogue above, Michonne had crept into the guest head and hid in the shower behind the tinted glass door. She had nothing with her except her little duffel bag.

Jus was scheduled to hail Peeler aboard Booty Call in three minutes.

Chapter 29
Leslie aboard her sailboat

Leslie was growing worried. More accurately, Leslie had played the worried card, and picked up the ace of frantic from the dealer's deck.

She sensed something was very wrong, and cursed herself for sending Avaline alone in search of that wild child. Ava should have been back by now, even to report that there was no sign of Michonne and that they should consider another avenue.

"That's it, fuck it!" Leslie cursed herself. "That's my child out there missing, who in turn is searching for yet another missing child. How the Hell…"

The sum of these parts did not add up well in Leslie's frazzled brain.

She picked up her cell and dialed 911, but before she hit the send button, she paused.

As well as she got along with Justin and Marlene, and as much as she trusted them, she wondered how much she really knew about their clandestine activities.

She whispered to herself, "Could they be involved with the mafia? Could they be caught up in this whole Florida drug trade fiasco?"

Leslie shut off her phone. No, she could not risk bringing the law down to these docks and having Jus and Marl direct retribution at her, or worse, Ava.

Plus, the cops might just arrest her for losing track of not only her own daughter, but also the young girl who was put in her care. That would be a tough one to rationally explain.

Leslie was a turtle on her back.

She decided that the only actionable move to was to embark on the search for her daughter. She would leave a note for Ava that instructed her to stay put in case she got back first, hopefully with Michonne in tow.

She began to shake, so she went below and poured herself a fat shot of Plymouth gin. "Fuck the lime!" she thought to herself while belting it down for fortification.

Chapter 30
Aboard Booty Call

Peeler stared at the ship-to-shore radio.

And stared some more, causing curiosity on the part of Jillian, who was growing impatient as to why these two were not wearing wetsuits and bringing up bales of Conzalez's precious contraband.

Jillian finally spoke up, "Hey, Mr. Peeler. What's with the delay? My uncle would not be happy."

To which he responded, "No delay, Miss Jillian. Just letting the Captain get his second wind before we go to work. He'll be topside anytime now. I'll start getting the gear ready in five minutes."

Peeler knew it was a lie. Justin was now two minutes past his hail time. This was not typical of Jus, who was meticulous in all aspects of every operation, and Peeler didn't know the half of it when one factored in Jus' previous Boston career. He knew that Shark would want to be awake for whatever happens.

With an overtly suspicious look from Jillian, Peeler went down below to alert Shark as to the situation. A few seconds later she could hear the two smugglers exchanging exclamations in alarming tones.

Shark came topside and grabbed the mic, "Free Lance, Free Lance! Come back to Booty Call!" He waited a seemingly life-time-long thirty seconds and pressed the mic's button again, "Free Lance, Free Lance. Come back to Booty Call. C'mon Justin, What's the story here?"

Again, only silence. Not even a crackle from a poor connection.

Shark slammed the mic back in its holder, "Peel! Secure all the gear and weigh the anchor. Hurry your ass! You still have the coordinates and heading? Shit, Peel. I roped them into this. Dammit!"

"Aye, Skip." Peel began his tasks at a feverish pace.

Shark gave it thirty seconds and then repeated louder commands into the mic, "Free Lance, Free Lance! Come back to Booty Call! Dammit Justin, where are ya?"

Without hesitation, Shark fired up the engines as Peeler was bringing up the anchor.

"Stop what you're doing!" yelled a livid Jillian. "Who do you think you are? You were hired to do a job, and dammit we're not leaving 'til it's done!"

This was punctuated by the 9-millimeter in her right hand aimed directly at Shark's head.

"You move one inch, Captain and I'll blow your brains across the Atlantic. Peeler will be next. Trust in that I am well versed in both shooting a gun and driving a boat. You two are merely strong-backed worker bee drones."

Bertolami had a major problem on his hands. Jillian was especially dangerous, and at the moment her beauty was not able to mask the true identity of both a trained killer and someone who would at any given moment, go to the grave for Don Conzalez.

Shark gulped, "Now, Miss Jillian. Be reasonable. Our friends could be in major trouble right now and their lives could be in danger, and I single-handedly put them up to it. We need to just blast out and check on them. I promise, once we know they're safe, we'll return to this spot and recommence our mission. I have our coordinates marked on the GPS, and those drugs aren't going anywhere. We have enough of a sample stash to prove that we found what Conzalez is looking for. This is just an unfortunate delay."

"I'll tell you what's unfortunate, Captain. You fucking up is what's unfortunate. Do you think I'm some dumb Spic slut? What's to stop you from sneaking the waypoint to your friends, and then have them call ahead to alert someone else who could beat us back here and steal what is the rightful property of my uncle. No, no, senor. We're staying here, and you and monkey boy are strapping those tanks to your pale white backs. As you were properly warned, I'm an ace shot. On the count of ten, I'll send a nick into the fat of your left thigh. Not a major injury so that you can't do your job, but effective for letting the blood seep out just enough to serve as a dinner chime for the reef sharks if you don't expedite your mission quickly."

Shark stared at the barrel of the pistol as Jillian made things clear, "I don't wanna do this, Captain, but Don Conzalez would completely condone my actions."

Jillian was then quiet while anticipating Shark's capitulation. Nothing happened, and Jillian re-pointed the barrel of the gun at Shark's leg, "Have it your way, foolish sea dog. Uno. Dos. Tres…" Suddenly, a bolt of thought shot through Jillian's mind.

She had lost sight of Peeler.

"AAAAAAHHHH!!! NO!"

A jetting clam-shot of hot crimson blinded Peeler's left eye as he plunged a fishing gaffe into Jillian's cervical spine. Immediately, she was half-paralyzed with his first twist. With his second wrench of the object, blood freely ran down her back and she dropped the gun and fell to her knees. She stopped uttering any sounds, but her eyes blazed toward the sky in disbelief until finally she fell face-first and smashed into a pile of rusty fishing reels. Old hooks pierced her cheek and dangled in drops of blood. With all of her intense concentration aimed at Shark, she failed to remember that Peeler was on the other side of her and could also be adept with the tools onboard a fishing boat.

Blood spilled across the deck, and Jillian died quickly with an open mouth and wide, E.T. eyes.

The immediate state of shock snatched away Shark's ability to articulate.

"Peel. What. Have you. Done?" Shark's mouth barely managed to emit. He then exhaled and stared into the horizon.

Wired on adrenaline, Peeler ran below and brought up some thick chain. He wrapped Jillian's once runway-model body in heavy lead.

"Peel, I cannot believe you're givin' this chick a Jacob Marley Wetsuit. I… can't believe this is happening. Can't bel…" The usually boisterous Shark softly uttered gibberish while still in a cloud of shock as he watched his long-time first mate wrap Jill's body like he was packing sausage.

When Shark regained composure, they together heaved her lifeless body overboard. After the initial splash, she sank quickly, and within a few minutes the two longtime partners noticed the first fin.

"Peel, my friend. We've been through a lot of shit. I mean a lot of shit over the years. However this time, we are sooo fucked! We're going to return not only without the bulk of Conzalez's drugs, but much more alarmingly, without his adopted fucking niece, who we just so happened to have fucking murdered!"

Peel gently held his hands steady and chest-high as to attempt to instill some calmness in his frenzied captain.

"Peel, the fact that it was self defense will mean shit to that old bastard. He will hunt us down from Nome to Rome, with the only instruction on the bounty will be to deliver just the heads."

Shark took a deep breath as Peeler rubbed his own neck as if imagining being headless.

"Skip, I know you want to kill me right now, but think of two things."

Shark stared in disbelief that Peeler was attempting to be the voice of reason.

"We still have the location's waypoint stored, so we're able to get back here anytime. Also, we really need to step on it and get to Justin and Marlene. They could be in even deeper shit, if that's even possible?"

"Okay, Peel. For once, you're making sense. Damn... Alright. Fuck it, let's go."

Shark barked at Peeler to hold on while he slipped the engines into gear. The madly focused Captain threw down the hammers, and the Booty Call blasted off in the direction of the last contact with Free Lance.

Chapter 31

Aboard the Free Lance

Hidden away in the guest head's shower, Michonne was now in a full-blown state of panic. She knew damn well that something very wrong was happening in the salon. The only voice that she now heard was a man's with a strange foreign accent. She was steadfastly determined to help Marlene and Justin, but was confused as to what to do and when to move.

The little girl's gut told her to hold tight to try and get a read on what was transpiring. She wished that she had that gun from target practice on the dock, but all of her worldly possessions at the moment resided in her travel pack. She didn't think that magic markers and candy cigarettes would be much help in this situation, and off-hand she could not think of anything else that might. However, she was hell-bent on offering assistance.

Several feet away in the salon, Khalil trained the Russian AK on his three prisoners. Madide finished binding their hands and feet with plastic zip ties that he had stashed in his baggy clothing, which like Khalil's cell, had also avoided frisk detection.

When Khalil was confident that the situation was well in hand, he turned to the three prisoners while making certain that the passengers were also paying attention, even if the majority had no idea what he was saying. Not that a verbal translation was required, for they clearly understood what was happening.

"Okay, crew and guests aboard the Free Lance. I, hereby as your new captain, am commandeering this vessel and everything on it including you. Justin, as I've heard your friends call you, your boat is now mine and in possession of my organization."

Justin was silent while clenching his teeth.

"I've tweaked our plan which is now to dump the passengers in some remote spot on the coast. They won't say a word to anyone for fear they'll face arrest and deportation. Good luck to them in your sewer of a country. What I do with you and your friends is still up for decision, but I guarantee that it will not be as accommodating."

Justin was internalizing every word.

"Madide and I will then proceed south on your boat where we'll rendezvous with our partners who are already well entrenched in your society. We have big plans, captain. Big plans. Our ideas are on a grand scale and most creative."

Justin spoke up without the slightest sign of fear.

"Whaddya plan to do, Khalil? You could at least indulge us as to your plans so I at least know what historical moment my boat will be a part of."

"Very well, captain. I must admit that my excitement is compromising my normal tendency to avoid boasting. I will indulge both your request and my temptation to tell.

"Think about this. Wouldn't it be fun to pack every square inch of this 50-footer and ram her into the side of the largest cruise ship in the world? And especially now during the summer season when the children will not be in their classes."

Marlene inhaled in horror.

"You Americans and your incessant obsession with our victory on September eleventh, and indeed, it was a glorious day for our cause. The last time I checked, the death toll was just shy of three thousand. Not a bad day's pay, as you cowboys like to say."

"Murderous bastards! Cowards!" yelled Marlene, "What are you, fuckin' al-Qaeda?"

Khalil slowly shook his head in contempt, "Woman, you people always want to attach labels. Keeps things easy for your feeble minds to comprehend. Good guys, bad guys. Cops and robbers. My dear lady, if it were only that simple."

Gerbil chimed in, "Whaddya gonna do, you bastard?"

Khalil simply smiled. "Since you ask, Mr. Gerbil, as I believe you are called. I will paint you a picture, as you have no chance of alerting anyone and shamefully I am gushing with excitement.

"The largest cruise ship in the world is the Orchestra of the Seas owned by the Prince Caribbean international cruise line. As we speak, the massive vessel is docked in Miami for two weeks of maintenance and upkeep before shoving off for ports worldwide.

"Captain Justin, picture a vessel so huge that it would take over two dozen of your large boats to equal its length. It weights an astounding 220,000 tons! As I mentioned, approximately three thousand people died on September eleventh. This massive vessel holds almost nine thousand passengers and crew! Captain, it's a floating American town!"

The vision of these numerical projections silenced even the always verbose Gerbil.

"And the beauty Captain, is that with the help of your boat's autopilot system, Madide and I will be able to watch the artful devastation from afar while sipping American liquor. Again Justin, we don't want to die anymore than you, but we do enjoy watching others provide the entertainment."

Justin snapped back, "You're out of your mind, Khalil. The port of Miami will be swarming with security and Coast Guard twenty-four seven to guard that ship."

Khalil smiled, "Of course, Captain. We would never waste your pretty boat on a futile operation and try to attack the ship at port. No, no. You see, you Americans have an amazingly arrogant false sense of security. Think of the multitude of buses, trains, subway cars, and yes, large cruise ships, that are left totally vulnerable once they leave their berths.

"Once that mammoth ship exits Florida coastal waters, fully loaded with western sinners who paid huge sums for a week of fornication and gluttony, it will be left virtually unattended. Yes, they will have radar and see your boat coming, but that of course will be scrambled by the most powerful and secret Russian Navy signal jammer that we could procure on the Mid-Eastern black market. It's all too easy.

"Our experts back home estimate the best time for a direct hit will be in the middle of the night while most of the passengers are either sleeping or fucking. Even with the unprecedented rescue operation that will be launched from the mainland within minutes, they predict a death toll of roughly two times that of September eleventh."

Khalil returned to the moment, "Until then, make yourselves comfortable. And don't try anything stupid, for the woman will be the first head to meet one of your galley blades unless Madide beats me to it with a blast from her own gun. We will stay here for a spell as we await our brothers who are coming aboard to inspect this vessel for what will be its best and most effective utilization. Trust that she will be fully fueled up and packed solid with C-4, TNT, RDX TATB, plastique, and perhaps even a few firecrackers for fun.

"For now, as you Americans say, sit back and enjoy the flight." Khalil smiled in his glory.

He then turned toward the passengers, "As for the rest of you, don't get any ideas of helping these infidels. They are not your friends. You are animal cargo to them, all in the name of their filthy American greed which will ultimately lead to the annihilation of their godless civilization."

It appeared that half of the passengers understood the warning, while the rest merely donned looks of confusion and alarm.

Khalil continued, "You are not part of this war. Just sit and be quiet. Yes, you are being delayed, but if you behave, you will be delivered unharmed to a shore destination not yet determined. From there, you are on your own in this so-called Land of the Free."

In the guest stateroom head, Michonne could only make out some of Khalil's words, but she knew that the situation was serious. She pleaded with herself to figure out a way that she could help. She owed Marlene and Justin her life.

Chapter 32
Aboard Booty Call

Shark had the throttles pinned and the boat was enjoying a mild set of following rollers which aided in their headway. They were making excellent time and would be arriving shortly at Free Lance's estimated location.

Shark knew that the approach angle would be crucial to avoiding detection. With darkness quickly setting in, Shark was going to have to steer toward Justin's vessel with no running lights.

Suddenly, an object appeared on the Call's radar. In his salty gut, Shark knew it had to be his friends. The object appeared to not be moving, which meant that they were either in a soft drift or anchored. Either way, it gave Shark many more approach options than if the vessel was fully underway. Instinctively, he suspected a problem, which was only confirmed by the several unanswered radio hails during the fifty-minute trip.

"Peel, I think we found 'em. I know that you've got Jillian's pistol, but go down below and snag something with a little more testosterone and range. Bring up the revolver for me. I'll keep manning the helm, but I need you in a sniper's position."

"What's your plan, Skip?" asked a nervous Peeler.

To which Shark responded, "I wish that I had the luxury of one, buddy."

Peeler obediently went on the hunt for the hardware as his heart begin to pick up its pace. Damn, he needed a drink...

Shark stared forward into the growing darkness while maintaining course and speed.

Chapter 33
Free Lance and Booty Call rendezvous

Khalil was busy yapping away on his cellphone in some indecipherable language. How he got that thing onboard was a frustrating mystery to Justin. As much as Jus wanted to feed them to the sharks, he had to admire their skills.

As if Marlene could read his mind she spoke up, "Justin, I'm sorry. I should have frisked him better. It's my fault."

"Marl, don't even go there. It's not anyone's fault. Captain Bleach seemed to have things under control. Everyone was on edge and in a rush to just get the second half of the operation underway," assured Jus.

Gerbil noticed the phone call as well, "Hey, Tak! You sneak that phone on board with it up your ass? Sure ya got plenty of room up there with the workout you get from those camels."

Khalil ignored him. He was engaged in conversation, but made a mental note that the big one with the sinner's mouth would die a most painful death.

Jus was deep in thought and shuddered at the vision of what horrific numbers of casualties would be caused by a boat his size packed with the right type of explosives and then rammed into the side of a large cruise liner. The tragedy would be greatly magnified if they knew to hit the target near where thousands of gallons of fuel were stored. He couldn't imagine the devastation.

Meanwhile, while Khalil did not realize that Shark and Peeler finally had a visual on Free Lance, it would be short lived unless they got closer due to the sun dropping like a stone.

Aboard Booty Call, Shark said nothing and was firmly focused on the other vessel's stern. The cockpit was vacant, and he saw nobody at the helm, which he did not interpret as a good sign.

"Peel. If anyone is aboard, they must be down below. Our approach should be from their bow to limit their visibility."

He cut the engine RPMs so that the boat was barely making way, but would be enough to maintain a course while keeping the Call quiet.

Khalil was still busy on the phone, so it was Madide who thought that he heard something outside.

He made quick eye contact with Khalil who immediately spoke in an irate tone and then shoved the phone into his pocket. He pointed the AK at the three prisoners and barked, "Madide, go up on deck and see if you're imagining things."

While the two hijackers were talking, Shark began an approach so that the two vessels would meet bow to bow.

He instructed Peeler to crawl out to the vessel's bowsprit with the 338 Lapua Magnum rifle that he found below. The range of the rifle was more than needed for this distance, but Peel loved its accuracy. The wind had abated and rollers diminished, which would contribute toward a clean shot.

Shark was quiet at the helm with Booty Call in neutral about thirty yards away from Justin's boat. Peeler was at his station, with rifle locked, loaded and trained on Justin's bow.

At first glance, the Free Lance appeared abandoned, but the seasoned Shark did not want to fall for anyone playing possum.

Shark whispered into the transmitter, and Peeler heard him clearly on the other end.

"Keep still and be quiet, Peel. As you can see, our visual is not great. It's getting dark and the damn haze is setting in. You don't want to go and shoot the wrong target."

Onboard Free Lance, Madide crept up into the stern's cockpit and saw nothing. He looked around, blind to the front of the boat, and saw nothing in the rear. He returned to the salon and reported to Khalil,

"There's nobody out there, Khalil. At least not in or toward the rear of the boat. Want me to check up front?"

"Yes," curtly responded Khalil, "But don't go up there so exposed. Go down below, and toward the front of the boat there must be a hatchway that you can pop and get a visual of what's in front of us."

"Got it," said Madide as he quickly hopped down from the salon. He passed the guest quarters and continued toward the main stateroom in order to find a forward hatch. As he proceeded, Michonne could hear him go by and could tell by his clothes' whooshing sound that he was alone. She tried to think of what she should do.

She looked down at her duffel bag.

She quietly unzipped it and sifted through the contents. There, all but forgotten, was the scalpel that she had used on Miner Redd from what seemed like another lifetime. She took it out and held it firm while scraping away the old molester's dried blood. She slowly crept out of the head and around the corner toward Justin's room where Madide was now opening the hatch to gain forward visibility.

Chapter 34
Shred's Hideout

After Shred figured that Avaline had been given enough time to calm down and have some refreshments, he instructed one of his goons to go fetch the child so that they may speak in private.

Two minutes later, Ava was brought into Shred's office where she was instructed to sit still in a beat-up, dusty easy chair.

The girl spoke first, "I want my mom. I want to go back to my sailboat and see my mother and make sure she's okay. I told you several times, I don't know where that little girl went. I tried to go find her but instead you kidnapped me!"

"There, there, now dear," Shred calmly spoke as he tried to diffuse Ava's fiery emotions. "Kidnapping is a very strong word, and certainly does not apply in this case. You've been made very comfortable and have had all the snacks and soda that you want."

Ava snapped back, "What I want is outta here! I want to be away from this place and these freaks. You all reek!".

Shred almost chuckled, for the girl had a point as to the cabin occupants' demeanor and aroma.

"Well, honey, then it's your lucky day. In about fifteen minutes, the boys and I are going to head down to the marina and bring you back to your sailboat. We might even stop in for a chat with your mom. Would that be okay with you?"

"Don't hurt her. Just please bring me home." said Ava as she instinctively knew to simmer down.

Shred responded in a forced calm tone, "We would not ever dream of hurting her. But you have to promise to be well-behaved when we go down to the dock. No yelling or crying. If you act like an angel, nobody gets hurt and we just get to have a short visit with your mom. You'll be there too, if that makes you more comfortable?"

Avaline paused, then replied, "You can't bring all these crazy looking guys. You'll scare my mom and more importantly, everyone else on the dock. Trust me when I say they won't like it for all of you strangers walking around looking all scary."

Shred rubbed his chin in thought, as the girl did have point. He definitely did not want to attract any unnecessary attention, especially from the members of Port Side Vow who were always wary as to the intentions of outsiders.

"No, no, my child. It's just going to be me and my good friend. I'll have him put on more presentable clothing. We'll be ready to go soon.

"Hey, Zoot! Show the kid where to wash her face and hands. Give her a towel and a Coke or whatever she wants. We're going to that marina."

"Yeah, boss," replied a cloudy-sounding Zoot. Shred figured that the idiot had been hanging around the gas shed again.

Chapter 35

Free Lance
& Booty Call

Madide popped the hatch and slowly raised his head to peer outside. He couldn't see clearly in the dark haze, but his instincts sensed a presence.

Meanwhile, on Booty Call, Peeler looked carefully through his rifle scope which gave him much greater magnification across the water than Madide's mere human eyes.

"Shark," Peeler whispered into his small mic. "There's someone crawling up from the Lance's forward hatch. Visibility is still tough and I can barely make him out, but he's definitely not a friendly. He's got wild, scraggly hair, kinda like an old Chuck Manson pic. Just let me know how you want to proceed."

"Roger, Peel." replied Shark as he put the boat in gear and inched closer toward the Lance's bow. Madide heard the sound and sensed movement, yet he did not dare yell to Khalil and risk exposure. He was stuck in a predicament from which he saw only one way out. He reached for the pistol and brought it up through the hatch and onto the deck. He switched to a more sturdy position so that he was standing on the foot of Justin's bed with his chest and head exposed to the open air and Peeler's rifle scope.

Peel saw the movement, and with the scope's telescopic assistance he saw that Madide was armed.

"Peel, what's going on?" asked Shark.

"Skip, the guy's got a piece, and although he's acting like he smells a fish, it seems like he can't really see us yet. Your call."

"Okay, Peel. Something is majorly wrong here. Odds are much in favor that whoever he is, he's not a friendly. There's no movement on the vessel, and Jus is not answering the ship's radio or his cellphone. This might be a mistake, but continue to monitor the target. Use your discretion, and if you sense a reason to take him out, then do what ya gotta do. We need to make a move here. We could be losing valuable time."

"Okay, Skip."

Meanwhile, Michonne crept into Justin's stateroom undetected by Madide. Gripping the scalpel, she walked toward the bed. There was just enough din from outside that Madide could not hear her steps.

Michonne inhaled deeply, and then grabbed Madide's ankle and slid the scalpel deeply across his Achille's Heel. The hijacker screamed an inhuman shrill and kicked wildly with his other foot, which barely missed Michonne.

Madide howled in pain, offering Peeler an easy target. Instantly, the first mate made a game-time decision and squeezed off a shot.

THUP!

Madide's head exploded like dynamite in a watermelon.

What was left of the hijacker dropped down through the hatch, bounced off of the bed and crashed in a thud on the stateroom floor.

Michonne looked on in horror, and quickly jumped into Justin's closet. She shut the door as quietly as possible, while keeping a hold on the scalpel that now dripped crimson.

Back in the salon, Justin quietly smiled as he heard the commotion. His instincts told him that it had to be Shark out there wreaking wonderful havoc.

Khalil was frozen. He was tempted to run toward Madide's

screams, but the complete silence that followed confirmed his death.

The terrorist looked at his three captives, while simultaneously warning the other passengers.

"Nobody. I mean, nobody is to move an inch! One twitch will be your last."

Jus, Marl and Gerb all knew that the best course of action right now was inertia. They were still cuffed and had no idea what was really going on, but whoever was assisting with the situation seemed to have the upper hand at the moment. Justin confidently sensed that Shark was playing a role, but whatever the case, he did not want to give Khalil any reason to start unleashing the fury of Gerbil's AK.

Khalil crept down the hallway toward the main stateroom, and he could already see a bloody tributary beginning to snake down the corridor. He stopped and listened for any sound coming from the salon, but was met with the bird-tapping of slight waves against the hull.

As he moved closer to the open doorway, he immediately saw the headless body of his partner sprawled across the floor. Madide's neck streamed so much blood throughout the room, that Khalil failed to notice that his friend's Calcaneal tendon had been severed, and that the mass of tissue resembled a ball of twine behind his knee cap. He assumed that the blood was all from Madide's missing head whose thief he was certain came from the outside, as the hatch was still wide open. He was oblivious to the fact that only a few feet away hid a scalpel-wielding little girl lying in wait.

Khalil remained silent and emotionless as he surveyed the scene. No sounds. No prayers. For Khalil knew very well that this type of ending was merely an occupational hazard. He had to plot his next move quickly. He still had three dangerous hostages upstairs, and now an enemy outside who had proven more than willing to kill. He had to formulate a plan fast, and what kept popping into his head was letting loose in the salon with the AK on his hostages and the so-called passengers. He could then grab the vessel's controls and blast across the water in hopes of a rendezvous with his comrades. It was a long shot, but it was the only avenue that seemed to make sense. He would select a course away from the enemy waiting outside, and would hope that his commandeered boat was faster than that of any pursuers.

Back in the salon, Justin noticed that Gerbil had been unusually quiet since Kahlil's departure. One might have chocked this up to Gerb being fearful, but Jus hoped from experience that Gerb might actually have an idea. While Justin was certainly capable of proving a deadly adversary, he was unfamiliar with assuming the quarry role. Gerb was more conditioned to winding up in jams where he ended up as prey.

Jus turned to Marlene trying to lighten the moment, "Hey Marl, I bet your classmates at Suffolk Law never would have envisioned you tied up at gunpoint due to your counterfeiting and human trafficking careers."

Marl forced a chuckle, "Oh, I dunno. They might be more apt to believe that then visions of me strutting around all day in yoga pants, sipping a Starbucks while heading to the Garden Club meeting."

Justin could hear a faint scratching sound, and whispered, "Gerb. What's up?"

"Jus, I'm sitting next to something sharp. It was sticking into my back and was annoying, but it might very well allow me to slice these plastic cuffs. I've been working at it for a few minutes, and I'm almost there."

"Careful, buddy. Don't give this nut any reason to dance with that trigger finger."

"Shh. Don't worry. Just another minute."

Marlene remained silent. While normally she could barely tolerate Gerbil's mongering presence, at the moment she was placing hopes in his will to survive.

Suddenly, a slight snapping sound came from Gerbil's lower back.

Chapter 36

Port Side Vow Marina

Shred and Zoot had cleaned up considerably well, and Avaline looked no worse for the wear.

"Now, dear," reminded Shred, "We're heading down to your mom's boat now. Remember, no running or yelling. We will bring you right to her and then just have a little chat."

"You promised not to hurt her. You promised!"

"She's going to be fine, dear. As long as you do as I say and remain calm and quiet."

The group walked seemingly unnoticed down the gangway and was only a few boats from Leslie's, when they noticed that the boat's back deck was empty.

Shred spoke first, "Avaline, dear. Could your mom have gone looking for you?"

"Maybe, Captain. She could be down below. Or maybe she went to the cops?"

To which Shred responded, "For both of our sakes, let's hope that she did not foolishly alert any authorities. Zoot, let's see if she's below deck. We all need to get out of sight, anyway."

As the trio boarded and immediately descended into the cabin, Avaline instinctively realized that the boat was empty.

"She's not here, Captain."

"Alright, kid," Shred paused in thought. "Sit down and relax. Zoot, keep an eye on her."

Shred searched the entire vessel to ensure its lack of occupancy.

A few minutes later after poking around, Shred was satisfied that the three were alone. The gangster sat in a fold-out deck chair, pulled out a cigar to chomp on, and took a deep breath and waited.

They sat in silence for what seemed like an eternity to Ava, when suddenly they heard footsteps on the dock and the clump of someone jumping onboard. Seconds later, Leslie appeared in the doorway.

"Ava!" cried the frantic mother who was shocked when it was her daughter who put her finger to her lips. She gave her mom the universal zip it sign with a jab from her other hand.

"What the hell is this? Ava, are you okay?" Leslie's glance darted about the room.

"Who the fuck are you?" she shot a look at Zoot, and then immediately at Shred.

The gang leader quickly tried to diffuse the panicked mother, "She's fine. Aren't you, dear? We had a little misunderstanding but she was well fed and properly taken care of, and voila! Here she is back home safe and sound."

Leslie's frightened look didn't waiver despite the bizarre calmness that her daughter was exuding.

"What is it that you want from me and my little girl? What could we have possibly done to get mixed up in any dock hoodlum bullshit?"

Shred motioned to Leslie as one would to ask a dog to sit.

"Ma'am. My guess is that you did nothing. However, we are interested in the activities of a couple of your dock neighbors and a certain little girl, younger than your daughter, who live on a large sportfish a few slips down. Now they are the ones who we'd like to have a word with. What do you know about them? Tell the truth, and tell it fast. If I am satisfied, I will ask you to take Avaline, get in your car, and go spend a night or two at that magnificent hotel on Bayview Ave. Accommodations and meals are on me."

Leslie remained still and listened with her head side-tilted and slightly raised.

Shred continued, "On our way down the dock, I noticed much to my disappointment that the vessel in question is unfortunately missing. Now, my sincerest recommendation is that you take me up on my generous offer and vacate the premises. My colleague and I wish to rent your pretty vessel for a brief period. Trust that she will not leave her berth."

Leslie appeared to slowly relax, albeit she maintained a wary gaze.

"Of course," warned Shred, "Your first temptation upon leaving will be to approach the authorities. Now, that would be easy enough to do, however please understand that one call to my crew will ensure that you will never cross the mainland causeway alive. Moreover, the authorities will be curious as to why you are in possession of a half-dozen kilos of cocaine hidden on your vessel. That's a stash worth… Oh, I dunno. Well over a hundred grand. Shit. Zoot, what's the Georgia prison term for possession with intent to distribute that much blow? Gotta be hefty with all of the new crackdowns. Pun intended."

Leslie's eyes immediately burst.

Shred was now having fun at taunting Leslie, "Hey, Zoot, how many cops we got on the payroll?"

"Dunno, boss. Maybe four, last time I checked."

Leslie snapped her head and shot back, "There're no dope on this boat!"

"Well, there is now, lady. And nobody will ever find it except a drug-sniffing hound. If you turn me over to the police, I will gladly inform them of the operation that you and I have been running. Yeah, maybe in the end they'll believe that the drugs were planted, but boy what a shit-show you'll have to endure. Not to mention the heat the whole circus will bring down on this marina. From what I understand of this place, some of your neighbors will not take too kindly to the attention that you'll attract. Based on reputation, some of these guys may very well decide to take the law into their own hands and punish you for your crimes. And I'm not sure if you even know how the coastal drug trade works? In any case, have confidence in the fact that your knowledge and presence during such commotion with be duly considered in whatever sentence is handed down by the court of dockside opinion. And of course, your daughter's role as a witness will be noted as well."

Shred sat back high in his chair with his chin raised, while chomping once again on the unlit cigar.

"Trust me when I say by far, the best course of action for you and your pretty girl is to go check into the hotel under my alias account. My credit is firmly in place and it's origin is a well-kept secret. All of your needs and expenses will be taken care of. All you gotta do is eat, drink and most importantly, keep your mouths shut! You'll await my instruction as to when it will be time for you to check out and return safely to your unscathed sailboat. Nothing will be missing from its contents with the exception of one nasty stash of contraband."

Shred paused for effect, and surveyed the room.

"From looking around, I can't help but notice that there appears to be few empty gin bottles, so the open bar component to my offer should alone be enticing."

Sadly, this sparked Leslie's attention.

"You have three minutes to pack a bag and calmly be on your way. Zoot will alert our plant-man at the hotel who you will find most cordial and accommodating. Enjoy your brief vacation."

Avaline finally interjected. "Mom, these guys might be nuts, but they're friggin' serious. Let's just go."

Clearly defeated, Leslie caved and responded after a deep breath.

"Okay we'll go. But may you rot with the devil, you filthy bastard."

Shred snickered and responded, "Yes, Hell. Lady, there is a corner suite with chilled champagne already awaiting my certain arrival."

Leslie grabbed a large hiking pack from the closet and went into the head to start grabbing their things. She knew that the creep was most likely bluffing about the drugs, but she thought to herself, "Fuck it. Coupla nights of luxury with an open tab doesn't sound that bad. I sure could use a drink."

Chapter 37
Aboard the Free Lance

Back in the vessel's salon, Gerbil had finally managed to snap free his bracelet and pulled out his cleverly hidden pocket knife to remove the feet clamp. He then quickly extricated Justin and Marlene.

Now they had the numbers, yet Khalil still held the AK.

After Justin gave the firm international S.T.F.U. signal to the passengers on the salon floor, he turned to his partners in a whisper, "Okay guys. That nut is somewhere down below. I don't hear anything, so most likely all the racket a minute ago means that the other one is dead and our hijacker is either in shock because of the scene, or is plotting his next move. My guess says the latter."

Marlene quietly spoke, "We have to take him fast, and hopefully by surprise. We can't just wait up here and let the prick gather his thoughts. Let's rush him and pray that he doesn't hit a vital organ. All we have aboard for stitching is the damned boat canvas sewing kit."

Gerb smiled, "Marl, I know that you're not some dandelion and can handle your weapons, but when's the last time you were around an AK that's spitting open-flair in a confined space? He could chop down the three of us in seconds."

Justin considered the situation, "Gerb's gotta point, but we've no alternative. We go now. Don't think, just move. Let's try and take some cover. Hopefully he's cornered in the main stateroom. You guys try and find space to hide, preferably on the starboard side where there's more room. If we play this right and get far enough down the hall before he notices, I can snag the Baretta that I have stored in a drawer on the portside wall."

Justin then fetched three steak knives from the galley.

"Here, Gerb." Jus gave the makeshift weapon to the big man who almost laughed.

"Jus, remember that line in The Untouchables?"

"Shut up, Gerb. Let's go."

Down in the master stateroom, as Khalil was texting coordinates and information to the rendezvous boat, Michonne remained a statue in the closet. She held the wet scalpel tight in her small hand, while doing her best not to make a sound. So far, Khalil was convinced that he was alone with the exception of the headless Madide.

Suddenly, Khalil could hear the sound of movement from the direction of the salon. He pocketed his phone and disengaged the AK's safety. He walked a few feet out of the stateroom and immediately raised his weapon, for the tall images of his three prisoners were suddenly standing ten feet away.

"Don't move," instructed Khalil as he brandished his weapon and noticed the knives. "You fools are going to strike me down with cutlery? Should I just mow you down now, or should I need to consider the value of keeping one of you alive? Perhaps the woman might provide added benefit?"

Justin stared into Khalil's crazed eyes as the hijacker continued.

"You see, the other passengers are useless for offering knowledge about navigating these waters. Hmm… The more I think of it, Captain, it is you who I may spare. You will of course, drop your petty weapon. Now."

"You don't give orders on my vessel, Khalil," calmly spoke Justin.

"Unfortunately, Captain, you don't have much choice. Where that leaves you is that you now have the pleasure of choosing which one of your playmates I slaughter first. Of course, they're both going to Hell, but you may pick the one who clears the path."

Justin was silent with stoic eyes, however deep down he was in a state of panic. He knew this guy had nothing to lose by killing Gerbil and Marlene.

Jus shot back, "Take me, you bastard. Let them live. They both know the water and how to run the boat. You're going to need both of them for any shot at success."

While Justin and Khalil continued their standoff, the height advantaged Gerbil could see over the hijacker's shoulder only to notice that the closet door behind him was slowly opening.

Khalil did not notice the immediate excitement in Gerbil's eyes. While Gerb had no clue who was in the stateroom, he realized that it had to be an ally.

Khalil continued, "Enough, Captain. Like in your cowboy films, I'm gonna count to ten. Then it's very simple. You will tell me which of your companions dies first. If you fail in making your selection by the count of ten, I will blast your right leg with a few lead pegs. It will be enough to require immediate amputation once the rendezvous boat arrives, but you will not die and your mind will remain in tact. One. Two. Three. Four…"

Michonne heard the exchange and knew that she had to act fast. With fire blazing in her normally still-water blue eyes, she opened the door just enough so that she could take two long steps. In a decathlon high-jump move, she leaped onto Khalil's upper back and firmly grabbed his forehead, while plunging her middle finger into his right eye.

Taken by surprise and engulfed in pain, Khalil screamed in shock and agony while the two fell backward onto the floor with Michonne being pinned by her wounded prey. Justin and company all ducked as the AK bullets began a Bellagio-like spray of fire into the hallway's ceiling. Justin used that split second to reach into the portside drawer and grab the Baretta.

Immediately upon landing on the floor with Khalil, and with her left hand still gripping the hijacker's face, Michonne's hand dug the scalpel deep into his neck and carved out his Adam's Apple with the precision used on Miner Redd several days ago.

Blood spouted from Khalil's neck like a grade school bubbler. Michonne then lost her grip and fell to her right side. Khalil's hands clawed at his blood-spewing neck.

Justin in an astonishing move driven by pure experience and primal instinct, aimed the Baretta at Khalil's head. With instantaneous surgical aim, the former assassin blew out the left side of Khalil's face in a precisely engineered shot.

The group froze.

"Michonne! My God... oh, my God! What are you doing here?!" screamed Marlene. All three partners were transfixed at the sight of the unassuming little girl, turned ninja.

Marlene knelt down and helped Michonne to her feet. She hugged and caressed the little girl as if she were a newborn.

A birth that was followed by a sanguine baptism.

Gerbil and Justin slowly approached. They took an undertaker's inventory of Khalil, and then approached Marl and Michonne who now faced each other and held hands in shock and disbelief.

"Hell of job there, kid. Shit..." said Gerb in his way of complimenting Michonne's performance.

Gerb then turned to Justin, for he was amazed at his instant accuracy of the shot, "Nice shootin' Tex."

Jus smiled and pretended to tip an invisible hat. "Much obliged. Just like riding a horse."

Justin then marveled at the blood-soaked little girl. He noticed a familiar look that he normally only recognized from his mirror. It was an undefinable vision of serenity.

Justin patted Michonne's head, "Great job, honey. I don't

know what to say except that I hope that someday you'll realize that you pulled off a miracle and saved over two dozen lives, not to mention thousands if these bastards executed their plan."

Justin then rubbed Marlene's shoulder and looked at Gerbil, "Alright, guys. We gotta mobilize fast. My gut tells me that upon going forward topside, I'm gonna find two friendly pirates aboard a fishing boat who will hopefully ask questions first before shooting."

Justin slowly walked down the hall and up the steps to the salon. As he passed the passengers, he gently instructed, "Okay folks, show's over. Why don't ya get up and stretch, but don't leave this room until everything is under control. Whoever needs the head, just hang on a coupla more minutes."

Some nodded in comprehension, while others continued to stare forward. With that, Justin grabbed a white towel from the galley and walked up on deck toward the bow.

Back aboard Booty Call, Shark and Peeler had heard the shots roar from Khalil's AK, as the front hatch in Justin's stateroom had remained open. Both of them were cautious to not immediately tie up next to the Free Lance for boarding until they got a firm handle on what was the situation's status.

"Peel!" Shark yelled out toward the vessel's bow, "Keep your binoculars trained on the Lance. Keep your weapon ready, but do not fire until we get the lay of the land. That was automatic fire, and now everything's quiet. I don't like the…"

Shark's communication to Peeler was interrupted by the sight of someone waving a white flag as he walked up the port side of the vessel. Peeler quickly recognized Justin, pushed his weapon to the side and stood up with his binocs dangling from his neck. He adjusted his vision and called out, "Justin! Hey man! You okay over there? What the Hell is going on?"

"Long story, Peel. Long story. Hey, yell back to Shark that all's cool. Come on over and tie up to my starboard. I'll ready the lines."

Peeler relayed the message back to Shark who was more than happy to oblige.

"You got it, Peel. Grab the lines." Shark slid the vessel into gear, and proceeded toward the Free Lance.

With both vessels made fast, Peeler and Shark hopped into Justin's cockpit. The three men exchanged hearty hugs and shoulder pats. Shark could tell that Justin was completely worn out, but the smile on his face gave the him hope that things were okay down below.

As they entered the salon, Shark and Peel immediately noticed the passengers corralled together. Some merely sat, while others were engaged in various stretching moves.

Shark looked at Jus, "While this is not a normal sight, by the smile on your face, I'm assuming Marlene and Gerbil are in one piece?"

"Yeah, man," responded Jus, "I have a lot to explain, but I'm going to have to do it fast, and all your questions will have to be reserved for the VHF on the ride home. We gotta quietly drop these passengers off ASAP somewhere safe on the coast, but definitely not near the marina. I know of a cove with an abandoned dock where they can beat it. There's a path that'll get them to a small downtown 'bout a half mile through the woods. After that, they're on their own - welcome to America. In the beginning of all this, I didn't care if they ended up as 'cuda bait, but after all the shit that's gone down, I hope they make it."

Jus used his fingers as a comb as he tried to think.

"We gotta get outta here. I need to get the boat back in her slip and cleaned without attracting any unwanted attention. It wouldn't take a forensic scientist to look in my stateroom and realize that something big-time nasty went down."

"Okay, Jus. But I'm afraid that Peel and I also have a major problem to deal with back on land. We're pretty much fucked and it involves a certain Don Juan Conzalez. I realize that you've had one Hell of a long day, but for us I fear Round Two is just beginning."

"Damn, Shark - I don't like the sound of that," said Jus, "In that case, let's get outta here soon. C'mon down below and check out Peeler's handy sniper work, as well as some other interesting pieces of art. Then, we'll blast off."

Chapter 38

Port Side Vow Marina

Shred's hotel plant reported that Leslie and Ava had checked in without incident. He and Zoot could now relax a bit and wait. Leslie had informed Shred that she had no idea as to Justin's ETA, but that it should not be long as per their last discussion.

Shred really had no idea how he was going to approach Justin and Marlene with the required level of stealth, but he knew that subtlety would be vital in not attracting attention. While Port Side Vow captains kept to themselves for survival, many were unabashedly nosy.

Every ten minutes, Shred instructed Zoot to go up on deck with binoculars and check out if Free Lance was approaching the harbor entrance, which was a half-mile from the marina. So far, the usually active waterway was quiet.

Until now.

Zoot dropped back into the cabin with the binoculars in his left hand. With his right he made sure that his shoulder gun holster was secured.

"Boss, it looks like boat will be here in about five minutes. There is another boat following close behind. Looks like they're cruisin' together."

"Alright, Zoot. Gather up our stuff and we'll await their arrival. There's a large ice storage hut near their slip. We'll take position behind it and wait 'til they tie up. Then, we'll know who we're dealing with, cause that big guy could be with them. Don't forget the hockey bag with the guns."

The two hoodlums quickly walked down the dock toward the hut. Free Lance and Booty Call were breaking the no-wake speed rule, and it was now evident that they were traveling in tandem.

"Zoot. Take position and stay outta sight. We need to observe them for a bit to get a head count and figure out our best means of approach."

As Justin laid the Free Lance against the dock to her starboard, Gerb and Marl cleated the lines to make the boat fast, prior to Shark tying up Booty Call to Justin's port. While Shark left his engines running for a bit while Peeler secured the two vessels, Justin killed his motors and went down below to use the head and to check on Michonne, which simultaneously rendered him out of sight from Shred and Zoot.

After a couple of minutes, Marlene broke out a case of water that was in one of the compartments. Shark and Peel hopped over the gunnel and into the Lance's cockpit, and the exhausted gang took swigs of the much the much needed hydration.

Shark spoke first, "Man, guys. This has been a long friggin' day. Marl, I can't believe what you guys went through. And to be saved by a little girl? Damn!"

Marlene sternly responded, "Yeah, Shark. Imagine a girl? A young girl who single-handedly saved the lives of over two dozen people, maybe thousands. Shit," continued a sarcastic Marline, "I'm surprised that she didn't crawl up in a ball and cry for her mommy the whole time."

"Yeah, no shit." responded Peeler, obviously not getting Marlene's point.

The four were quiet and rested for a minute. Justin and Michonne were still down below and out of sight.

Gerb spoke up, "Hey Marl, thanks for the water and all, but it's warmer than donkey piss. Where can I snag some ice?"

"Ice would be great, Gerb. You can grab a couple of bags from the chill hut down the dock."

Gerbil hopped off the Lance's starboard side and turned left. While he walked slowly due to his fatigue, it was fast enough to alert Shred and Zoot to the fact that they better figure out a strategy and a quick way to execute.

"Zoot, let's grab him and take him hostage. Make sure the Magnum is loaded and ready to go."

"Boss, I ain't scared or nothin', but damn, he's one big bastard! Can't we wait to see if the chick walks down here, or even the scrawny guy from the other boat?"

"Wish we could, but it's no time to get choosy. Get ready. I'll grab him and pull him behind the shed, and you dig that piece in his face fast so he doesn't try any tricky shit. Got it?"

"Got it, Boss. I'll be quick so nobody notices."

The two gangsters waited for their target to get close enough for a pounce. Shred had regrets in not bringing more of his guys, but he was grateful that as of now they were not grabbing attention. The sheer sight and smell of his crew when gathered in one place, without fail attracted a lot of curiosity and swiveled too many heads.

While Shred was deceptively strong for his size, under normal circumstances he would have been no match for the massive frame of Gerbil Turner, however the gangster's target at the moment was borderline delirious from lack of sleep. Shred also had the luxury of surprise.

Gerbil reached for the door of the hut,

"Wha!"

Shred grabbed Gerbil from the big man's left side and quickly pivoted to swing him around to the back of the ice hut. As Gerbil turned from the force of Shred's lightning attack, he was immediately met with the barrel of Zoot's Smith & Wesson .357 Magnum revolver. Zoot shoved the gun between Gerbil's teeth so that the big man was forced to swallow half of the barrel.

Shred put his finger to his lips as he looked Gerbil up and down. He quickly frisked him and said, "Okay, big fellah. You're gonna introduce us to your friends, but before you do you're going to let us in on all the fun secrets that you selfish pricks have been keeping from us."

Gerbil stared in shock.

"So, start talking and keep your voice low, or so help me, Zoot here will blow your melon clean off. Now, what've you people been up to?"

With Justin and Michonne still below deck, Marl and the other two guys were chatting and unwinding. It was Marlene who first felt a tingle of alarm.

"Hey guys, it's a solid bet that Gerb got lost on the way back from getting ice, but I got a weird feeling. I don't hear him singing his usual dirty songs, or feel his Frankenstein steps. Call me paranoid but we better take a look."

Marl yelled down to Justin, "Hey, babe. The guys and I will be right back."

"K, Marl," Jus yelled back up.

Justin was busy moving the bodies of the dead hijackers, while Michonne sat on the floor resting, when they both suddenly heard Marlene scream.

"Shit! No!"

Justin's immediate reaction was to run up to the open cockpit, but as he quickly looked at Michonne, he realized that he might want to survey the situation before blowing his cover.

"Be still, stay quiet," said Jus.

Michonne nodded her head in confirmation.

Justin peered out of the stateroom's starboard window and looked toward the left from where he thought he had heard Marlene scream. He tilted his neck and could see two dirty, rough looking guys face to face with Marl, Shark and Peeler. One had a gun buried in Gerbil's mouth and had handcuffed his wrists. The other guy seemed to be barking the orders and had instructed the others to get on their knees. While there was some distance between the Free Lance and the ice shed, Justin was able to make out the voices once he slowly slid open the window.

The robbers or whoever they were, thought Justin, had the advantage of not only being armed, but also because this part of the marina was somewhat remote and out of sight of most of the other members.

Shred stepped back and assessed the situation.

"Okay, my new found smuggling friends. Your Wookie partner, who at the moment is not very eloquent, gave us a small taste of what you shit-dogs have been up to. And right under my nose? No, no. This is not acceptable. You see, like any other civilized and functioning society, we have trade regulations that are put in place to ensure that business and commerce flow smoothly, and are transacted in a professional and proper manner."

Marlene spoke up, "You're nothing but a cowardly thief and bottom feeder! Too much of a pansy to take on the big guys in Atlanta, so you lurch in the weeds in search of bread crumbs to steal. I bet you sit down when you pee."

Shred leaned forward and gave Marlene a slap across her cheek. While her head jerked to the side, she quickly returned her eyes pointed straight at Shred.

It was all Justin could do not to crawl through the window and strangle Shred to death with his bare hands, however he knew that there was a better way out of this. He could not believe that this was happening all over again.

Justin motioned to Michonne to stay put while he went into a large closet on the port side halfway between the master stateroom and the steps to the salon. Michonne heard him sifting around, and then returned with a weapon that made Michonne's jaw drop. She had never seen anything like it. Justin never used it while teaching Michonne target practice, and it resembled an action movie prop.

Just took a cloth and rubbed his .300 Win Mag bolt-action sniper rifle. It was one of the favorites used by the famous American sniper, Chris Kyle. It was also was one of the weapons of choice of an equally skilled Boston assassin who did everything possible to avoid any sort of notoriety, and who currently held the beast in his hands.

Justin checked the chamber, and Michonne was wondering what he was doing by moving around different pieces of the intricate weapon.

Looking satisfied, Justin said to Michonne, "Stay put, dear."

"No!" she hissed, "I'm coming with you."

Justin paused, but caved, "Okay, we're going to the end of my bed. You sit on the floor. I'm gonna peek outta the forward hatch to see if I can get a field of vision."

Justin placed the large rifle on the bed and slowly crept his head out of the hatch, when his eyes were immediately met with a nightmarish vision.

"Now," said Shred, "You're going to tell me where exactly on which of your boats is the money that you received when you picked up your cargo. I know that there's cash, weapons and other objets de valeur on board your vessels. And I want it all! And I'm taking it now! That will serve as an installment payment toward what you ultimately owe me in port tribute, which I will calculate once I get a proper handle on your operation's scale."

In a show of defiance, Marlene spat on Shred's shoe which did not at all faze his momentum.

"So, my friend Zoot here is going to blow this big man's head off in ten seconds if you don't tell him where you're hiding your booty. If there are safes onboard, I want the codes. Now."

The mood tensed as Shred began a slow count. Zoot held the Magnum deeper into Gerbil's mouth, whose eyes now bulged out of his head. Shred continued the count as the three others were still on their knees and remaining firmly silent in defiance of Shred's order.

"Shit!" Justin said quickly and quietly. "Dammit, they're calling his bluff. What the hell are they thinking? Fuck! No!"

Jus was about to reach down to prepare a shot, when he heard the screams and yells from his friends. Shred had reached a ten count, and Zoot with his free hand smoothly slid a gleaming sharp industrial kitchen knife across Gerb's neck. He sliced so deep that the former security officer's head easily fell backward and down past his shoulder blades.

Gerbil tasted the copper-flavored blood on his tongue a half-second before his body registered any feeling. He wasn't scared until that split second of realizing that he was seeing what was behind him. After that, he only felt death.

Any color in the faces of the others vaporized at the unconscionable horror they were witnessing. None could utter a sound as their eyes floated in a daze.

Gerb's lifeless body lay on the dock, and a maroon stream flowed into the still marina water.

Zoot calmly wiped the blade on his pants, and then pointed the Magnum at the other three who were still on their knees.

"So," Shred said nonchalantly, "You thought that I was bluffing. Yeah, you know me. Just a small-timer. A bottom-feeder. Isn't that right, pretty lady?"

Marlene could not reply, as shock had snatched any ability to move or speak. Peeler's urine darkened his entire lap, as he too was also floating in a zombie-like haze. Only Shark maintained composure and firmly focused on Shred's hollow eyes.

Shred stared at the trio, "Time is getting short, folks. I'm growing weary from your stalling."

Shred took Zoot's knife which despite being wiped, still seeped Gerbil's blood, and walked over to Marlene. Zoot trained the Magnum on the two male prisoners, while Shred grabbed Marlene's hair and pulled it back in order to have plenty of room to rest the razor sharp blade.

"We're gonna try this again, folks," Shred said calmly to Shark and Peeler. "Gentlemen, this time I'll count more slowly, for I want you to really consider what you're about to witness. The responsibility for this tragedy will be tattooed on your conscience for the rest of your miserable days. Now, provide me with all the information that I requested, and I will refrain from not just slitting this pretty dove-white throat, but also from cutting her fucking head clean off!"

Justin had to move. This guy was unraveling, and losing it fast.

Jus grabbed the rifle and hoisted it up through the hatch. He laid it gently on the deck, and took a wide visual to ensure that nobody else was on their way down the dock. Fortunately, all was quiet. He picked up the Win Mag and peered through the scope, which at first cast a wide angle. He had the whole scene in his sights, but the vision of Marlene in the scope shot a searing pain straight down his back and he suddenly felt woozy. He was breathing heavy, and his thoughts wandered. He kept wandering and breathing, as his thoughts drifted off…

Justin noticed that each inhale jabbed at his throat with a cold sting. His face went numb as he succumbed to the frigid blizzard air. Long cascades of white streamed through his clenched teeth. With every heave of the thick snow, his muscles grew tense and the shovel handle began to slowly crack.

Just a few more scoops of snow and he would complete the path and find a way out. He needed a safe escape route in order to save everyone. The only chance was for him to dig this path through the quilt-layered snow. The ebony sky presented neither sun nor moon to aid with navigation and progress. Before him was an endless fog.

"Be careful of the pretty ferns, Daddy. Don't hurt the ferns when you shovel."

Justin heard the little voice behind him, yet when he turned, all he could see was a vast sea of white.

"That's Fern Valley, Daddy. Ferns live there. A seagull lives there too. He is pretty, but only has one leg, Daddy. They are our friends. They feed our minds bits of snow and chocolate Easter eggs. The ferns can guide us. Don't hurt the injured seagull, daddy. Don't hurt the ferns and the seagull with that big shovel. Do you have his other leg in your pretty bottle, daddy?"

Jus merely stared ahead into the horizontally falling snow.

Flakes stung his face like metal peppercorns, as he screamed into the gray abyss,

"Uncle Rick! No, Uncle Rick!. Why did they kill you, Why?!

"I'll get those bastards. I don't care if I have to slay the whole world, for it's mine to destroy in your name. The servant will be the master. The master is Death. I am Death - the destroyer of worlds! I will suck the life from everyone I touch. All I need to do is touch!

"It's easier to kill than to love. Easier to kill. Love kills, Uncle Rick. Love kills!"

Justin suddenly once again heard that same innocent voice from behind him, "Yes, Daddy. Love kills. Love kills, and we'll all be killed. Everyone dies in the end, Daddy. Can you kill me Daddy?"

Jus suddenly freed himself from the nightmarish daydream. He was sweating through his clothes and his breath was short. A panic attack was wrapping him like a blanket and he started to hyperventilate.

He left the rifle on the deck and slipped back down through the hatch.

He regained composure as Michonne silently looked on with obvious concern. She could tell something was wrong with Justin for his hands were shaking, but she instinctively knew that she should not speak. The little girl had no idea of Justin's former resume, and while he was always kind and gentle to her unlike most of her foster parents, she sensed a certain kind of pain which constantly afflicted Justin. When he laughed, even in her still developing mind, she knew that it was not the laughter of a gentle heart. Rather, it was the crazed laughter of a caged animal who only briefly felt a glimmer of freedom. His were memories that clawed at walls, within a mind held with shackles.

Finally, Justin regained composure and spoke, "Michonne, dear. I need you to do me a favor. No, actually, Marlene is the one who really needs the favor."

Michonne eagerly spoke up, "Anything. Anything for you and Marlene. Just name it."

Justin could not believe what he was about to ask, but in his way it was a gift to her. A present that nobody else could bestow upon her. It was the gift of allowing her to slay a dragon from her past that constantly roamed in her growing mind.

"Honey, do you remember when we played target practice and you shot that plate?"

"Yes, Justin!" she eagerly responded, "That was so much fun. Can I do it again sometime?"

"Yes, dear. You can actually do it right now. You see, there's a very bad man out there. I know that you've met bad men before, and I know that you taught one a lesson that he deserved."

"Yeah. There was a bad man that I had to visit before I came here. I did teach him a lesson. I kilt him. I kilt him real good."

"Okay, dear. There's a man out there who is going to hurt Marlene if we don't protect her. The rifle that I brought from the closet is right up on the deck. I need you to pretend that the bad man's head is that old plate. Can you do that? Can you shoot that plate again and save Marlene?"

"I-I guess I can try. I'd do anything for Marlene. She's nice to me. I don't want a bad man to hurt Marlene."

"Okay, honey. Step up on my shoulders. Go up through the hatch. Hold the rifle and look into the scope, just like you did the other day during target practice. Aim at the bad man who is trying to hurt Marlene. Make it so that he cannot hurt her or anyone else ever again."

Michonne swam in the instructions and immediately was atop Justin's shoulders. She reached across the deck, and slowly lifted the rifle. For most little girls, the weapon would have felt too heavy, but for Michonne it was as natural as holding a baby doll with marble eyes.

Meanwhile, Shred continued to slowly count, "Seven. Eight…". All was still and quiet except for the struggled weeping words uttered from Marlene, "Don't… tell… him…an-thing. Nut-hing…"

"Nine…"

Michonne, with the placidity of the one-legged seagull sitting twenty feet away who was licking his feathers, squeezed the trigger.

BLAM!!

The kickback from the powerful rifle jerked Michonne's body, but Justin anticipated such and had braced her with his arms and neck.

The fireworks show that was once Shred's head burst into tiny pieces that the dock crabs would savor for days. Zoot immediately turned, and his eyes stretched their muscle integrity with horror and shock. For an instant, a headless Shred stood calmly in place. A second passed, and he fell to the ground.

That was all the time that Shark needed to leap up and lunge at Zoot who was easily tackled. Shark spun the shocked henchman on his back, grabbed the knife and severed Zoot's jugular. As the blood began to stream, Shark quickly stuffed the upper half of Zoot's body into the water to avoid as much mess as possible, with Shred having already managed to soil the scene.

"Peel! Get to the boat, fast! Grab a scrub brush and some anchor chain. We're on borrowed time here! Move!"

While in a total haze of shock, Peeler immediately processed his captain's orders.

Back aboard Free Lance, Michonne and Justin had collapsed on the stateroom's bed. Neither said anything for several seconds.

Finally, Justin raised his upper body and hands so that he could prop the little girl upright. He looked out of the cabin window, and quickly turned his attention back to Michonne.

"Justin. Did I smash the plate? Did I make the bad man go away?"

"He's good and kilt, honey. And most importantly, you saved Marlene."

Upon hearing the confirmation, Michonne stared back at Jus with a bright smile. The Boston assassin, who up until now was firmly convinced of his inability to love anyone, would never forget that glance from the little girl whom he had grown to love as his own.

From now on for Justin, it would not only be an empty mirror that looked back.

Chapter 39
Free Lance's Salon

Marlene Dunn was beyond exhausted. Marlene Dunn was in a profound state of shock. Most of all, Marlene Dunn could kiss the now filthy floor of the vessel's once-cozy salon at which she had been staring for the past ten minutes. She finally looked up at Justin and Shark.

"Where's Peeler?" she asked with words that were barely audible. She still could not shake the gruesome sight of Gerbil's half decapitated head lopping over his shoulders as she helplessly watched. While she couldn't stand being around the big guy, she never would have wished upon him such a wretched ending.

"Peel's okay," responded Shark who desperately felt the need to break open one of Justin's bottles of anything, yet refrained.

"He's out stealing anchor chain from some dock boxes. I told him to sink those two bastards right where they fell. It's a pretty secluded area of the marina, and even at low tide there's enough murky depth to keep them hidden. Plus, the crabs and bait fish will have them pecked away soon enough. Eventually, a bull shark will smell 'em and make quick work of the rest."

Justin patted Shark's shoulder and then walked over to Marlene. He ran his fingers through her hair and kissed the top of her forehead with a most loving touch.

"Marl, you know that we can't stay here. Shred's people know where he's supposed to be. And Leslie? Shit. Who knows where the hell she is and what she's capable of blabbing. The poor lady probably thinks that Michonne was kidnapped."

Marlene exhaled deeply as Justin laid out the short-term plan.

"Anyway, we're not long for this place. I know that you're exhausted, but I'm tossing the lines in twenty minutes. We'll anchor up in some hole for the night and make for the Bahamas in the morning. We gotta get out of U.S. waters and plot our next move."

"Justin! What about that cruise ship in Miami? Holy shit, we need to alert the coast guard of those bastards' plans! I mean, they failed this time, but who's to say they don't have a backup crew with a Plan B ready to be executed. We can't just ignore that fact."

"No, of course not. After we get a few miles offshore, I'll use one of our burner phones to put a call into Carl Hiaasen at the Miami Herald about that ship being in danger. They won't be able trace the call's origin like if I called the FBI direct. Then, I'll toss the burner into the drink. While he's not law enforcement, Carl's got the connections to get the word to the right people. They're going to have to take it from there with the Coast Guard."

Marlene slowly nodded.

"That's all we can do, Marl. We can't risk getting exposed. Any of us, and that includes Michonne. The last time I checked, I don't think we want her in the limelight in case anyone ever finds that swamp rap with the missing voice box. Right now, we need to plot out our short-term strategy."

Marlene sat up with a jolt, "Speaking of Michonne, I hope that your plan includes her being aboard?"

"Of course, Marl. While she won't exactly be leading a Anne of Green Gables lifestyle, I'm confident that we can show her a better world than where she came from."

Shark piped in, "All your talk about throwing the lines reminds me. Shit, I gotta screw too. Won't be long before Conzalez sounds the alarm after he realizes that his niece is missing and she ain't comin' back. If he ever, ever, catches up with yours truly? H-O-L-Y shit! It will make your hijackers' endings look downright merciful."

"Shit, man. You think he'll put out one of his famous top shelf contracts?" asked Jus.

"Yeah, Jus. Unfortunately, I do." replied an overtly nervous Shark.

Marlene looked confused, "Guys, what's a top shelf contract?"

Shark turned to Marl, "Sister, it's when ol' Juan throws the usual hundred thou bid out to the open market. He then adds a footnote with two requirements, that if satisfied, will double the purse. That means you get the really big money only if you deliver the just the head to Conzalez in a little bow and ribbon box. You're then required to leave the rest of the body in a visible location, preferable hanging from an A1A overpass. That serves as a reminder to other pricks like me of the consequences of crossing the Don. Thus, he only wants to be served the top shelf, while the rest of the world drinks the rot-gut."

Marl was abnormally speechless, but finally asked, "What's gonna happen to Peeler?"

Shark sniffed the air, "Ah, shit. Peel's an unknown. No real marquee value in the marketplace. Certainly not worth much to the Don. Ol' Peel will most likely just end up in a wood chipper in the 'Glades. Gonna hurt, but gonna be quick enough. Hopefully, they'll show mercy and let him belt down a bottle first."

All three let the air grow still.

"Where you gonna go, man?" asked Justin.

"I dunno," responded an unusually nervous Shark, "We can't head south. The guy has eyes everywhere from Bimini to Barbados. Shit, I gotta think. Maybe cruise north up the coast and tuck in where we can without bringing heat. Hell, maybe we'll head up to your hometown and toss the anchor there. You now anyplace with soft beds in Boston? Perhaps you could set Peel and I up with a couple of gals of compromised virtue?"

Jus appreciated Shark trying to make light of a dire situation, for everyone was swimming in a panic pool.

"Yeah, brother," smirked Justin, "I still have a pretty hefty Rolodex for the old town. Damn, I miss the place. Funny about Bostonians. No matter where we go, and whatever shit piles we step in, we always yearn to get back. Y'know? Smell the franks at the Sox game. Feel the chilly Spring nor'east breeze over the Harbor. Hear the screech of the T…"

Jus snapped back from the thoughts in his head and turned to Marlene.

"Babe, I'm gonna go check on Michonne," Jus said as he proceeded down the steps toward the main stateroom.

The little girl was curled up in Marlene's favorite blanket and merely stared at the starboard window.

"Hey, honey, you okay?" asked Jus. "You did an amazing job today. Saved all our lives, and helped get rid of some very nasty men. I'm so proud of you", said Justin as he kissed the side of her head.

"Thanks. I'm glad that I smashed that plate."

"Me too, honey." responded Jus, "Me, too."

The little girl said as she tilted her head, "But, I'm mostly glad that you believed that I could do it."

Jus continued to smile, "Never forget the words, Whoever gives up on me, never believed in the first place."

Michonne slowly nodded as she processed his words and locked them away.

He sat on the bed next to her as she sat up and stretched. She took a gulp from her water bottle and took a deep breath.

"That plate broke in so many pieces." she said with a slight chuckle.

Justin could only admire how tough she was. He marveled at the strength and tenacity all packaged in one little girl. He wanted to show her a great world, and hopefully a life whose lessons might be learned from teaching by example of what not to do. For Justin had a lengthy list of stark memories to share.

It was Jus' wish that with a little coaching and love, while forever capable, Michonne would not have to smash too many more plates in her days ahead. Those times that he hoped would be shared with he and Marlene.

Jus turned to her, "By the way, honey. I gotta ask where you learned the carving technique that you used on Khalil's neck? Not that I want you making a habit of such a move, but I must admit that it was downright artful."

This was Justin's twisted version of a father/daughter moment.

Michonne paused and flipped through her memory, "I'm not exactly sure, but I used to carve little animals out of wood, and got really good at it when I lived with the meanie Narios. But it also learned it again here on that cooking channel I like."

Jus nodded his head as he marveled at her description.

"It's a fun show where this big loud, happy guy is always nice and cooks pretty meals and jokes around. He's always telling funny stories, and when he gets excited and yells, 'BAM!' I laugh every time. One day I watched him teach the audience how to slice scallops. I guess that's how I learned it."

Justin slightly shook his head with a smile, patted her on the head and said, "Rest easy, dear. Try and nap a bit."

Michonne slowly rolled over and looked back up at the starboard window, and quickly noticed a one-legged seagull glide by.

Epilogue

Worn out tires crunched and scattered a half-dozen chipmunks who were nibbling on a two-day dead rabbit in the corner of the Port Side Vow Marina parking lot.

The 70s B-movie Cadillac was overdue for a permanent check-in at the scrap yard, but its driver would just assume that he hit the boneyard first.

While it had taken several months, through his Boston drug-trade contacts and incessant arm twisting, the old dog was finally able to track down his bone. He hated to resort to the occasional drug running operations, which he considered a dirty business and well beneath his C.V. However, he did enjoy the vast network of people and information that it provided. The sphere of influence and valuable database created by the enterprise spanned far past the Quincy Quarries. He often chuckled at how he now at his advancing age, felt worldly.

The dirty white car door flew open, and out stepped Justin McGee's worst nightmare: Boston's own underworld legend, Darby McBride.

Old Darb had cashed in a lot of favors to get this far. Despite how clandestine Justin thought that his counterfeiting operation had been functioning, the nautical community is worse than a Penn Dutch sewing bee. Information and gossip carried gold bar weight, and the open market was never discriminatory with whom it dealt.

Never in a million years would Justin believe that the old bastard could track him down on the Georgia coastline. He figured that D.B. Cooper would be found first.

Darby walked to the edge of the lot and hid behind the thick bushes. With broken binoculars he scanned the marina, only to find snuggled in a corner a boat that fit the description that had been sold to Darby.

The vessel sat still. It was as if nobody was aboard, however a few seconds later a lanky, weather-beaten guy carrying some kind of chain hopped into the boat's cockpit, dropped the metal strand and went inside.

Darby would patiently monitor the scene from afar, but for only so long. He knew from vast experience that it was almost impossible to sneak up on Justin McGee, and he who tried did so at his own peril and only got one chance.

If one is to strike the King, it had best be lethal on the first try...

The old gangster walked back to the Caddy and popped the spacious trunk. Inside was a mini arsenal of weaponry that could outfit a small special forces unit.

He was proud of his accumulated array of deadly toys, and as he perused them, he finally selected one that he knew would prove to be the most accurate.

And the most painful...

Acknowledgments

Thanks so much to everyone at WWC in Vermont, with special shouts out to Uncle Steve, Ben, Dede, and Charita.

My appreciation to all of the bookstore owners and librarians who have supported my projects, with special thanks to Eric at Yellow Umbrella, Caitlin at Where the Sidewalk Ends and Amy and Lydia at the Eldredge Library, Chatham.

To William Martin and Capt. Linda Greenlaw, two consummate professionals (not to mention amazing authors!) who believed in me early on and have been forever generous with their guidance and support.

To fellow rockstar authors Art Vanderbilt II, Beth Splaine and Carrie Regan, to whom I am grateful for always being there as a sounding board and source of encouragement.

To the Fitzpatricks and Pollards everywhere who believed in my work and had my back during the challenging times.

For Heidi, Willy and Warnock for rooting me on during the Matriarch Game project.

For Kailee and Nicole, I pledge my love and support every time, everywhere.

Most of all I am forever grateful to the readers. Without you, Justin McGee would be relinquished to a solitary life of poverty and obscurity.

Cheers.